2018成都第二届国际诗歌周组委会　编译

时间深处的城市

——外国诗人笔下的成都

四川民族出版社

图书在版编目（CIP）数据

时间深处的城市. 外国诗人笔下的成都：汉、英 / 2018成都第二届国际诗歌周组委会编译. -- 成都：四川民族出版社, 2019.8

ISBN 978-7-5409-8551-6

Ⅰ. ①时… Ⅱ. ①2… Ⅲ. ①诗集—世界—现代—汉、英 Ⅳ. ①I12②I227

中国版本图书馆CIP数据核字（2019）第169460号

SHIJIAN SHENCHU DE CHENGSHI——WAIGUO SHIREN BIXIA DE CHENGDU

时间深处的城市——外国诗人笔下的成都

2018成都第二届国际诗歌周组委会　编译

出 版 人	泽仁扎西
责任编辑	秦　琳　李　娟
外文审读	卓　霞　林泉喜
责任印制	谢孟豪
出版发行	四川民族出版社
地　　址	四川省成都市青羊区敬业路108号
邮政编码	610091
成品尺寸	145mm×210mm
印　　张	9
字　　数	300千
制　　作	四川胜翔数码印务设计有限公司
印　　刷	成都市金雅迪彩色印刷有限公司
版　　次	2019年8月第1版
印　　次	2019年8月第1次印刷
书　　号	ISBN 978-7-5409-8551-6
定　　价	50.00元

《时间深处的城市——外国诗人笔下的成都》

编译委员会

时间深处的城市

\ 序言 \

时间深处的城市

中共成都市委常委 宣传部部长　田 蓉

“两江珥其市，九桥带其流。”成都历史悠久、文化灿烂，是中国首批历史文化名城和中国十大古都之一，拥有4500年城市文明史，2300年建城史，千年城址不迁、城名未改，孕育出“创新创造、优雅时尚、乐观包容、友善公益”的天府文化，成为推动成都繁荣发展的深沉力量。成都，是中国最具发展实力、创新活力和开放魅力的城市之一，连续10年蝉联“中国最具幸福感城市”榜首、连续5年蝉联“中国新一线城市”榜首。这座独具文学底蕴、独特文化魅力、独有生活美学的国际化都市，已成为世人所公认的“来了就不想离开的城市”。

文运同国运相牵，文脉同国脉相连。中华民族伟大复兴引领城市崛起，成都厚重博大的文化根脉在新时代正焕发出蓬勃的生机活力。特别是党的十八大以来，成都以坚定的文化自信和文化自觉，奋力建设“蜀风雅韵、中国风范、国际风尚”的世界文化名城，努力打造中华文化传播高地、国际文化交流互鉴高地。成都人既礼敬历史、挚爱传统、传承文化，也拥抱现代、面向未来、发展文明。成都人坚守中华文化立场，传承中华文化基因，大力弘扬中华文化独一无二的理念、智慧、气度、神韵，着力推动天府文化创造性转化、创新性发展，加快文商旅体融合发展，全力建设世界文创名城、赛事名城、旅游名城和国际音乐之都、美食之都、会展之都的“三城三都”品牌。2017年，成都正式成为继香港、上海、深圳、台北之后中国第五个世界文化名城论坛成员城市。

诗歌，是人类智慧的结晶，是文学王冠上的璀璨明珠，是时代的火炬之光和号角之音。中国是诗歌的国度，在五千年的中华文明史中，中国诗歌以独特的艺术品质和深厚的精神力量，表现生命，洞悉心灵，描绘世相，留下一批批脍炙人口、彪炳史册的诗歌佳作，成为中华民族贡献给人类的精神财富和文化宝藏。“有诗心的人多了，就充满了诗情画意。”千百年来，成都本就是一座有诗脉、诗魂、诗意的城市，这座城市的“血管”一直流淌着诗歌的基因。“自古诗人例到蜀”，历史上的伟大诗人几乎都到过成都或是在成都生活过。“九天开出一成都，万户千门入画图”——这是诗仙李白眼中的成都，“锦城丝管日纷纷，半入江风半入云”——这是诗圣杜甫眼中的成都，“濯锦江边两岸花，春风吹浪正淘沙”——这是诗豪刘禹锡眼中的成都，“晓出锦江边，长桥柳带烟”——这是放翁陆游眼中的成都……古代诗人前赴后继地铺陈与浸渍，成就了成都诗歌强大而充沛的气场。

为深入贯彻落实习近平总书记关于繁荣发展社会主义文艺的一系列重要讲话精神，继承和弘扬博大精深的中华文化，传承和发展独具魅力和气质的“天府文化”，以成都悠久的诗歌文化传统赋予天府文化更广阔、更深厚的内涵和价值，推进成都与世界诗歌的深入交流，促进全面体现新发展理念的国家中心城市建设，打造和提升成都作为新型世界城市的文化软实力。在成都市委、市政府，中国作协以及人民日报海外版的关心指导下，成都市文联连续成功举办了两届国际诗歌周活动，先后共有100多位与会的中外诗人，为成都创作了诗篇，留下了宝贵的文化财富。活动的成功举办，受到社会的广泛关注，赢得诗坛的一致好评，产生了较好的社会效益，使成都这座“诗歌之都”更加名声远播。诗歌正成为成都人的一种生活时尚，也成为成都又一张靓丽的城市文化名片。今年九月，我们将迎来第三届“成都国际诗歌周”的举办，开放、热情的成都，在此欢迎世界朋友们的到来。

当前，成都正以习近平新时代中国特色社会主义思想为指导，全面深入贯彻落实党的十九大精神和习近平总书记对四川及成都工作系列重要指示精神，确定了成都新时代“三步走”战略目标，并全力以赴地将成都建设成为世界文化名城，建设成为国家重要的文创中心、国际文化交流高地。我们相信，世界的成都，诗歌的成都，一定有着更加美好、璀璨的明天！

City in the Depth of Time

Member of the Standing Committee, CPC Chengdu Municipal Committee

Director-General, Publicity Department, CPC Chengdu Municipal Committee

Tian Rong

"Here is a city girdled by two rivers wearing a bracelet of nine bridges. " This city has Chengdu as its name which has never changed since its founding 2300 years ago while its civilization could be traced further back to 4500 years ago. Acknowledged as one of China's First Cultural and Historical Cities and Ten Ancient Capitals, its ancient history and brilliant culture have nurtured a new Tianfu Culture of being initiative, innovative, elegant, and accessible, empowering the city in progressive economic and social prosperity. The unique literature embedment, cultural charms and colorful lifestyle of Chengdu have put the city itself on top of China's Happiest Cities for 10 consecutive years and China's New First-tier Cities for 5 consecutive years. Believe me, the globalizing Chengdu is a city to which you would grudge to bid adieu.

The cultural status of a country is closely related to the past and present of the nation. Deeply rooted in profound culture, the city of Chengdu is witnessing a mushrooming vigor in this new era of China's Great Rejuvenation. Reinforced with cultural confidence and cultural reawakening since the 18th National Congress of the Communist Party of China, Chengdu is striding ahead in its construction of an international metropolis celebrating local cultural features of Sichuan, cultural identity of China as well as cultural achievements of the world. We are fully committed to making the city a reservoir of Chinese culture and a destination of international cultural exchanges. While paying great respect to history and with deep love for tradition, we are pledged to promote human culture through embracing new developments in the future of human civilization. Assured of our heritage of Chinese cultural genes and our perseverance in Chinese cultural stand, we are devoted to the reinvigoration of the philosophy, scope and spirit of the unparalleled Chinese culture. We will spare no efforts in our creative transformation of the Tianfu Culture. By way of pacing up concerted development of culture,commerce and tourism, Chengdu positions itself as a chosen city of high-end international cultural innovations, sports events, tourist attractions and a capital of international music festivals, gastronomic marvels and branded conventions. All those qualified Chengdu of its membership in 2017 into the World Cities Culture Symposium.

Poetry, crystal of human wisdom and pearl of literature, is the torch as well as the trumpet of its times. China, a nation of poetry, has made great contributions to human civilization with generations of poetic genius. Chinese poetry, with poetics and philosophy of its own, illustrates life, illuminates souls, and brings to life social proceedings. It has created a legacy of poetic masterpieces which have gained undying popularity on everybody's lips and prominence in history, as well as considerable spiritual wealth and cultural treasure presented by the Chinese nation to mankind. "Poetic romance comes into full bloom when there are more people with poetic minds." For thousands of years, Chengdu in nature has remained a city rich in poetic traditions, poetic souls and poetic elements. There has always been poetic DNA in the genetic code of the city. Furthermore, few great poets in China had not visited or lived in the city of Chengdu. Proof could be found in the following four poems about Chengdu by influential poets throughout the Tang and Song dynasties .

In the Celestial sphere Chengdu towers high,
It dwarfs ten thousand mansions under the sky.

—Li Bai

With songs from day to day the Town of Silk is loud,
They waft with winds across the streams into the cloud.

—Du Fu

Riverside blooming flowers beautify the land,
The vernal breeze exhales a stream of golden sand.

—Liu Yuxi

At dawn I passed by the River of Brocade,
The willow trees exhale cloud, Skyward bridge is made.

—Lu You

Thanks to the contributions by generations of great poets, Chengdu's poetry has gained strong and rich vibes.

To thoroughly implement the spirit of a series of important speeches by General Secretary Xi Jinping on the cultivation and development of socialist culture and art, to inherit and promote Chinese culture, and to foster and renew the Tianfu Culture with unique charms and characteristics, Chengdu is to leverage its long-lasting and rich poetic cultural traditions to enrich the Tianfu Culture with broader and deeper essence and values, by means of developing comprehensive indepth exchanges with international poetic community, thus making the city a national center that reflects new development concepts as well as a brand-new world-class metropolis with cultural enrichments. Under the guidance by CPC Chengdu Municipal Committee, Chengdu Municipal People's Government, China Writers Association and the Overseas Edition of the People's Daily, Chengdu Federation of Literature and Art Circles has successfully organized the International Poetry Week twice consecutively. More than 100 Chinese and foreign poets contributed their verses to Chengdu, leaving precious cultural treasures for the city. The event was so successful that it gained considerable spotlight from the public and the poetic circle, and it also generated positive repercussions in society, which has further boosted Chengdu's reputation as a city of poetry. Poetry now is becoming common pursuit among Chengdu people, as well as a magnetic cultural highlight for the city. The 3rd Chengdu International Poetry Week is around the corner this September. An open and passionate Chengdu is looking forward to the coming friends around the globe.

At present, upholding Xi Jinping Thought on Socialism with Chinese Characteristics for a New Era, as well as comprehensively and thoroughly implementing the spirit of the 19th CPC National Congress and the General Secretary's important instructions on Sichuan and Chengdu's development, the city has defined for the New Era a "three-step" strategy—that is, making big strides in building itself up as a world-class cultural city, a national key hub for cultural creativity, and a highland of international cultural exchanges. It is believed that Chengdu, city of the world and city of poetry, will be favored with a prospective future!

目　录

时间深处的城市

Amir Or

阿米尔·欧尔

Israel's famous contemporary poet and translator, born in Tel Aviv in 1956, is the author of eleven volumes of poetry in Hebrew. His poems, translated into more than 40 languages, have appeared in poetry journals, anthologies, as well as in 15 books in Europe and America. He is the recipient of several Israeli and international poetry awards, including the Pleiades tribute (SPE 2000) for having made "a significant contribution to modern world poetry", the Fulbright Award for Writers, the Bernstein Prize, the Levi Eshkol Prime Minister's Poetry Prize, the Oeneumi Literary Prize 2010 of the Tetovo Poetry Festival and the Wine Poetry Prize 2013 of the Struga Poetry Evenings. He has published eight prose and poetry books which he translated from other languages into Hebrew. In 1990, Or co-founded Helicon Poetry Society and later on served as Helicon's Chief Editor and Artistic Director.

阿米尔·欧尔，以色列当代著名诗人、翻译家，1956年出生在特拉维夫。已有11本诗集用希伯来语出版。其诗作被翻译成40多种语言在欧美国家的报刊上发表并被收入15部欧美诗选。其多次在国内外获得重要奖项，如“普勒阿得斯世界现代诗歌重大贡献奖”“美国富布赖特文学奖”“美国伯恩斯坦文学奖”“以色列总理列维·埃西科尔诗歌奖”“泰托沃诗歌奖”“斯特鲁加诗歌节葡萄酒诗歌奖”等。他已将8部外国散文集和诗集翻译成希伯来语。1990年，欧尔与他人联合创办了赫利孔山诗歌学会，并担任学会刊物主编和艺术总监。

__王浩/译

Chengdu's Watermarks

I

Daybreak in the alley
The street cleaner is sweeping
Heaps of yesterday

II

On the bank of the stream
The poplar dips its tip
Into the lake of the sky

III

An arrow of chirps
Above the poinciana tree

Where, birds, are you off to?

IV

Inhaling, exhaling

A full moon

The night is breathing

V

Night on my bed

The smell of your body

Doesn't fall asleep

成都的水印

一

小巷黎明时
环卫工已在清扫
昨日的堆积

二

溪水岸边上
杨树垂下的嫩尖
轻蘸天湖水

三

凤凰树枝头
欢鸣声如箭射出

鸟儿飞何处?

四

吸气又呼气

一轮满月悬空中

黑夜在呼吸

五

夜在我枕边

而你脉脉的体香

却没有入睡

—王浩/译

Andrea H. Hedeș

安德里娅·海德斯

Andrea H. Hedeș (February 23, 1997, Dej, Cluj County, Transilvania, Romania) is a Romanian poet, essayist, critic, publisher and journalist, with a degree in Cultural Studies at the Babeş-Bolyai University of Cluj-Napoca. Known for her work in the literary review field, she is also recognized for her poetry books. Her poetry evolved from the ludic, humorous and avant-garde style to a refined equilibrium, a great sensibility and an exquisite artistic intuition. Her poetry reflects the pursuing of the sacred, of the transcendent, turning the poems into a privileged place for spiritual aspirations and meditation upon the eternal problem of life and death, love and the meaning of man existence. Her literary criticism, proposing a pluridisciplinary approach of the literary text, contextualizing the book and its author.

安德里娅·海德斯，1977年2月23日出生于罗马尼亚川西凡尼亚克鲁日县，是罗马尼亚诗人、散文家、评论家、出版商和记者，在克鲁日巴比什·波雅依大学获得文化研究学位。她因从事文学批评而闻名，其诗集也获得了一定的认可。她的诗歌风格从诙谐、幽默和前卫，演变为高雅的平衡、极大的感性和敏锐的艺术直觉。她通过诗歌反映了对神圣和超越的追求，赋予诗歌以特权——对生命和死亡、爱情和人类生存意义的永恒问题进行精神诉求和冥想。其文学批评，提出了文学文本的多学科方法，为文本及其作者提供一定的背景参考。

__马丹/译

Chengdu, o amintire

Ai văzut munții?

M-au întrebat.

Nu, munții nu i-am văzut.

Ai văzut marea?

Nu, marea nu am văzut-o.

Spune-ne despre flori și animale,

Despre păsări și oameni,

Spune-ne cum vine toamna

În orașul cu turnuri înalte,

Cu ceainării de-a lungul râului șerpuind.

Despre acestea nu am ce să vă spun.

Și atunci m-au rugat și m-au implorat.

O, cum m-au implorat!

Spune-ne tot, spune-ne totul.

Totul? Asta pot să vă spun...

...munții se desprinseseră și urcaseră în cer

Împrumutându-i culorile,

Marea, care se arată ochiului iscoditor

În zilele senine,

Ca prin farmec, se înălță și ea în cer

Învățându-l să foșnească,

Orașul devenise rotund și cu totul și cu totul de aur

Și se așeză la locul lui dinainte pregătit

Acolo, sus,

Cu toate ale lui,

Și toate ale lui păreau o poveste,

Și era o altfel de toamnă,

Fără început și fără sfârșit

Iar vechii maeștrii ai poeziei

Și tinerii poeți

Compuneau poezii.

Fiecare poezie devenea cântec

Fiecare cântec, pană de aur...

Așa ceva e cu neputință, au zis,

Așa ceva nu putem crede,

Apropie-te

Și spune-ne acum adevărul,

Au poruncit,

Privind cu mânie în jur.

Se făcuse liniște

Și se făcuse seară

În aer plutea

O pană de aur.

Chengdu, a Memory

Have you seen the mountains?

They asked me.

No, the mountains I did not see.

Have you seen the sea?

No, the sea I did not see.

Tell us about flowers and animals,

About birds and humans,

Tell us how does the autumn falls

In the town with tall towers

With teahouses along the meandering river.

I have nothing to tell you about these.

And then they ask me and they beg me.

Oh, how they beg me!

Tell us everything, tell us all!

All? This I can tell you about...

...the mountains have detached and ascend into the sky

Borrowing its colours,

The sea, revealing herself to the inquisitive eyes,

During serene days,

Also lifted up in the sky,

Magically,

Teaching it to rustle,

The city has become rounded

And entirely of gold

And settled

In its place already set up for it,

Up there,

With all its belongings,

And all its belongings seemed fairy tale like,

And there was

A different kind of autumn

There,

A never starting and never ending autumn.

And the old Masters of Poetry

Together with the young poets

Were making poems,

And every poem

Was turning into a song,

And every song

Into a golden feather...

This is not possible, they say,

Such things we can not believe,

Come closer and speak the truth,

They ordered

Looking around in anger.

It was getting dark

And it was getting quiet,

Floating in the air

There was a golden feather.

(Translated by Andrea H. Hedeș)

成都记忆

有人问我，

你见过那儿的群山吗？

不，我没有见过。

你见过那儿的大海吗？

不，我没有见过。

和我们说说花朵和走兽，

飞禽和人情，

和我们说说镇上的巍巍高塔

和蜿蜒河流边上的点点茶馆

是怎样迎来秋天的。

关于这些我都没什么可说的。

于是人们询问我、恳求我。

啊，他们恳求我！

我们想了解那儿的一切，我们想了解那儿的一切！

一切？那我可以告诉你们在那儿……

……山峦兀立，高耸入云。

海天一色，

波澜不惊，

面对好奇的眼神，大海坦然自若，

偶尔也会涌向天际，

神乎其技，

传授着冯虚御风的秘籍。

这座城日臻完善

披着金辉

安常履顺

在那早已为它打下的江山，

那儿有，

它的一切，

它的一切都宛如神话一般，

那儿有，

一个截然不同的秋天，

那儿有，

一个从未开始也不曾结束的秋天。

古时的伟大诗人

和现今的新兴诗人

在一起作诗，

每一首诗

都化作一首曲，

每一首曲

都化作一簇金色的羽毛……

他们说，这不可能，

我们不会相信这些，

他们带着怒气

对我要求说，

靠近些，说实话。

暮色四合

万籁俱寂，

空气中飘浮着

一簇金色的羽毛。

__马丹/译

Antonio Wehrli

安东尼奥·威利

"Structurism" and "Flow" artist. He was born in Zurich, Switzerland and now lives in Luodai Ancient Town. He has successfully planned and held many art exhibitions.

安东尼奥·威利，“结构主义”和“流动”艺术家。他出生于瑞士苏黎世，现居洛带古镇，为洛带古镇客家文联书画专委会委员。他曾成功策划并举办多次画展。

__唐为之/译

My Paintbrush Lives in the Language of Luodai

Luodai, from Shu to Modernism
People flock through your streets
Fresh in spring with flowers beautiful
Warm in summer, spices taste hot
Cool in autumn, packing up for winter
Wait and hope for the sunshine of the New Year

Nearby the mountains, persimmon and peach
The flowers amaze, all come to see
Ximei its top, a peak like others
Comrades together cut by Tu River
Here I enjoy the life of Hakka
Here I experience friendship and hospitality

我的画笔住在洛带的语义里

洛带，从古蜀入梦现代
穿过街场，人头就攒动起来
我窥见暖春里你斑斓的花朵
盛夏里你火辣的邀约
你在天高云淡的秋天迎接寒冬敲门
回眸企盼来自新年的一米阳光

花儿为我绽放，争先恐后探头探脑
山的那边，是遍野奔跑的桃和柿
高高的山顶，巍峨峻拔
蜿蜒的洛水，割不断的乡愁
在这里，我混迹客家人惬意的生活
在这里，我感受到别样的情谊与热情

__唐为之/译

Barbara Pogačnik

芭芭拉・波加奇尼克

Barbara Pogačnik (1973-), is a Slovenia poet, translator and literary critic. She graduated from l'Université catholigue de Louvain in Belgium and completed her MA at l'Université de paris (la sorbonne). She has published four poetry books: *Poplave* (Inundations, 2007), *V množici izgubljeni papir* (Sheets of Paper Lost in the Crowd, 2008), *Modrina hiše / The Blue of the House* (2013) and *Alica v deželi plaščev* (Alice in the Land of Coats, 2016). Her selected poems are translated into Romanian by the poet Linda Maria Baros (Funia Luni Iunie), into French (Éléments, lieux, animaux) by the poet Stéphane Bouquet, her poetry has been translated into 28 languages. She has participated in more than 50 different literary manifestations all over the world.

芭芭拉·波加奇尼克（1973—　），斯洛文尼亚诗人、翻译家、文学批评家，毕业于比利时天主教鲁汶大学，并在巴黎索邦大学获得硕士学位。目前已出版4部诗集，即《洪水》（2007）、《人群中散失的纸张》（2008）、《蓝色房子》（2013）和《爱丽丝在服装国》（2016）。她的诗选被诗人琳达·玛丽亚·巴洛斯译为罗马尼亚语，被诗人史蒂芬·波桂译为法语；她的诗歌已被译为28种语言。她曾出席世界各地举办的50多个不同的文学活动。

__赵文希/译

Chengdu

Chengdu, tvojih nebotičnikov
je toliko kot dežnih kapelj v dnevu nad mestom.
Ljudje kot svetlobni srhi
polnijo in praznijo ta visoka skladišča življenja
in v prostoru zmanjkuje listja in trave.

Kot rumenjak v jajcu iščemo stari center mesta
os, hrbtenico, šivanko v kupu sena.
Iz nekdanjih časov je ostal
le usločeni most, ognjeni zmaj mesta.

Na mizah se šibijo jedi, ki v grlo naselijo zmaje.
Milijoni ljudi, ki se po mestu gibljejo tiho
in v njihovi duši se morda bočijo starodavni mostovi.
Postajajo telo velikega luskastega zmaja, ki se pregiba nad
pokrajino in srečno odpira rdeča usta.

V Chengduju otroci ždijo v naročjih staršev kot male pande
in izbrani pojejo zvonko kot prosojni lampioni.

Starodavna umetnost kaligrafije preseva skoz papir
kot nostalgija za minulimi hišami s privihanimi brki streh
strtimi kot pomladni hrošči s svetlečimi krili
in nevidno raste v času kot nadarjeni otroci.

Chengdu

Chengdu, your skyscrapers
are as many as the raindrops in a day over the city.
People, like shudders of light
fill up and empty out these high storehouses of life
the space runs short of leaves of trees, leaves of grass.

We search for the old town like for the yolk in the egg
the axis, the spine, the needle in the stack of hay.
From the ancient time all there is left
is the vaulty bridge, the flaming dragon of the city.

On tables abound the dishes settling dragons in the throat.
Millions of people drift silently through the city
and in their soul there might be ancient bridges arching.
They are becoming the scaly body of a giant dragon bending over
the landscape and opening happily its red mouth.

Babies in Chengdu hang in the lap of their parents like little
pandas
and become children singing with bright voices of translucent
Chinese lanterns.

The ancient art of calligraphy shines through the rice paper
printed as nostalgic for the deceased houses
crushed glossy bugs with jewel wings
nostalgic imperceptibly growing in time, like talented children.

(Translated by Cheng Yishen)

成　都

成都，你的摩天大楼
多如城市上空一天的雨滴。
人流，像光的震颤
注满又排空那些生活的高级店铺
那地方缺乏树叶，草叶。

我们寻找老城就像从鸡蛋里寻找蛋黄
从干草堆里寻找轴，脊椎，针。
从古代留下的无非
是这个城市的拱桥，火红的龙。

桌上摆满了盘子，龙卧在正中。
成千上万人沉默地飘过这个城市
他们心里可能有古代的桥拱。
他们正在变成一条巨龙，鳞片状的身体盘曲在
风景之上，兴奋地张开鲜红的大嘴。

成都的婴儿像小熊猫悬在他们父母大腿上
成长为用透明的中国灯笼般的明亮嗓音歌唱的孩子。

书法这种古老艺术通过宣纸而闪光
被印成对阴宅的怀旧
压碎了长着宝石般翅膀的光亮虫子
怀旧在时间中不知不觉成长，就像神童。

__程一身/译

Denis Mair

梅丹理

American poet, translator, holds an M.A. in Chinese from Ohio State University and has taught at University of Pennsylvania. He is currently a research fellow at Hanching Academy, Sun Moon Lake, Taiwan. He translated autobiographies by the philosopher Feng Youlan （Hawaii University Press） and the Buddhist monk Shih Chen-hua （SUNY Press）. His translation of art criticism by Zhu Zhu was published by Hunan Fine Arts Press (2009). He has translated poetry by Yan Li, Mai Cheng, Meng Lang, Luo Ying, Jidi Majia, and many others. He also translated essays by design critic Tang Keyang and art historian Lü Peng for exhibitions they curated respectively in 2009 and 2011 at the Venice Biennial.

梅丹理，美国诗人、翻译家，俄亥俄州立大学中文硕士，曾担任美国宾夕法尼亚大学讲师，现任台湾日月潭涵静书院研究员。他曾翻译哲学家冯友兰的自传（夏威夷大学出版社）以及和尚施陈华的自传（纽约州立大学出版社）。他翻译朱朱的艺术评论，2009年由湖南美术出版社出版。他还翻译过严力、麦城、孟浪、罗英、吉狄马加等诗人的作品。此外，设计评论家唐克扬和艺术史学家吕澎分别于2009和2011策展威尼斯双年展后写的文集也由他译介。

__王浩/译

Black and White Animals

—after a visit to the Panda Propagation Center in Chengdu

In Mother Nature's gallery when I walk down a corridor of colors
I am dazzled to see white and black appearing on a single creature.
The zebra's coat has stripes of black and white in alternation;
As for the orca, its white belly is set off from its ebony back
To manifest a streamlined yin-yang symbol, or a racing design.
Is there a message I'm missing, or am I just perplexed?
Because I know, for sure, something strange is going on.
The white coat of the snow leopard has rosettes of black
Not spots, with white hairs marking off the black sectors
And black hairs pepper its white coat, but do not gray it.
The panda is flopsical-mopsical; its big white head is marked
By black eye patches, in which its eyes are a bit off center
And its black limbs are hitched like trousers to a white torso.
The orca lives in the sea; the zebra on the savanna;
The panda in forests; and the snow leopard in mountains

A whale, a big cat, an ungulate, and a throwback bear
Their phyla and habitats are as different as can be.
With stripes, dapples, contours or whimsical color blocs
Taken together, they show a lovely range of styles
In their ways of combining two elemental colors.
Is there a message I'm missing, or am I just perplexed?
Because I know, for sure, something strange is going on.

黑白两色的动物

——访成都大熊猫繁育研究基地有感

在大自然母亲的展馆里沿一条彩色的走廊前行

我惊讶地看到黑白两色在同一只动物身上呈现。

斑马的外衣上有交替的黑白条纹；

虎鲸洁白的肚腹与乌黑的脊背泾渭分明

宛如一个线条流畅的太极图，或是某种赛跑的路线图。

我是否错过了某个信息，又或只是心生迷惘？

因为我知道肯定有离奇的事情在发生。

雪豹的白衣上印着黑玫瑰花朵

而不是黑斑——黑花瓣镶着细细的白边

而白衣中洒着黑毛，但没沾染出一片灰色。

熊猫呆愣又憨厚，白色的脑袋上敷着两片

没贴得很正的黑色的眼贴

黑色的肢体像是白色的身躯上套着四只裤腿。

虎鲸游弋在海中，斑马奔跑于草原

熊猫蹒跚在丛林，雪豹浪迹于群山：

一条巨鲸，一只大猫，一只有蹄动物，一只熊的老祖
它们的种属和居所实在天差地别。
它们有各自的纹理、斑条、轮廓、随意的色块
它们将两种基色做各自不同的搭配
展现出各自可人的风格。
我是否错过了某个信息，又或只是心生迷惘？
因为我知道肯定有离奇的事情在发生。

—王浩/译

After Visiting Zhuge Liang's Shrine

Through the ages, in collections of literati works
Anyone who made a trip to Chengdu
Would leave a poem about Zhuge Liang's shrine.
The 2017 "Chengdu International Poetry Week"
Arranged a salon-style gathering for us there.
Indeed the feel of the place is quiet and secluded.
I recall that Du Fu wrote it had towering cypresses;
But I was listening to the guide and forgot to look.
The tour guide summed up Zhuge Liang's era:
In a trifecta of kingdoms, upstart heroes contended.
She worshipfully directed our gaze to Liu Bei's statue:
Lordly and hugely tolerant, bent on restoring the Han.
A listener needled her: Was he a legitimate successor?
She stressed Zhuge's loyalty, a wizard who crowned his age
Moved by Liu's selflessness, he left his mountain idyll.
A heckler quipped: in chaos Liu was someone to rally around.

At any rate, seeing a historical figure treated so devotedly
Helped to establish a solemn atmosphere for our salon
Because a man straddled the line between human and divine
But his apotheosis happened in the past, and now this place
Has been restored as a venue for humanistic gatherings.
From human to divine to human, it was all an aesthetic process.
This kind of conversion gives a taste of the literati ethos
Which is why joining in this salon felt like coming home.

谒武侯祠后

古往今来，在文人作品集里
每个旅行到成都的人
都会留下关于武侯祠的诗。
2017“成都国际诗歌周”
为我们安排了一场沙龙式聚会。
感觉这地方确实安静隐秘
我想起杜甫写过这里有古柏；
但我只顾着听导游却忘了看。
该导游总结诸葛亮的时代：
在三国争霸、群雄并起中。
她崇敬地将我们的目光引向刘备的雕像：
忍辱负重，一心恢复汉室。
一个听者数落了她：他是合法继承人吗？
她强调诸葛的忠诚，冠绝一代的奇才，
被刘的无私感动，毅然出山。
一个诘问者俏皮地说：在乱世刘是个聚众自立的人。

无论如何，看到一个被如此钟爱的历史人物
有助于促成我们的沙龙一种庄严气氛
因为一个人跨在人与神的分界线上
但他被神化发生在过去，如今这地方
已变成人文聚会的场所。
从人到神再到人，这就是审美活动。
这种转变显示了文人精神的趣味
因此参加这个沙龙就像回家一样。

__程一身/译

Dinu Flămând

迪努・弗勒门德

Dinu Flămând, e poet roman. S-a născut în 1947. In timp ce scrie poezie traduce mari poeţi, precum Fernando Pessoa, César Vallejo, Borges, Carlos Drummond de Andrade, Umberto Saba, Samuel Beckett, Pablo Neruda ş.a.m.d. Pentru opera sa vastă a obţinut numeroase premii şi distincţii, între ele şi Premiul Naţional “Mihai Eminescu”. Volumele sale sunt traduse în franceza, spaniolă, germană, portugheză şi engleză.

迪努·弗勒门德（1947— ），罗马尼亚著名诗人。他翻译过佩索阿、巴列霍、博尔赫斯、安德拉德、萨巴、贝克特、聂鲁达等大师的作品。已出版《醒与睡》（2016）、《布拉格之春》（2017）、《阴影与峭壁》（2017）等几十部作品集。曾获得众多奖项，其中包括米哈伊·爱明内斯库国家奖。

__高兴/译

Saltul poetului Du Fu

Să-i adune laolaltă într-o mare casă
pe toți învățații lumii (care prin definiție sunt săraci
și n-au casă)
visa cu ochii deschiși poetul Tou Fou,
după ce vântul îi smulsese acoperișul de paie de pe colibă
iar ploile și foamea și frigul și dumurile cele lungi
ale exilului îi tociseră ființa care se tot micșora în lăuntrul lui.

Nu știa că dorințele pot deveni perfide
când uneori destinul le împlinește,
deci a plecat dincolo răpus de o mizerabilă
indigestie
după singura lui masă copioasă
dată tocmai în onorea repatrierii sale.

Acum statuia lui ne face cu ochiul

când îi vizităm somptuoasa casă unde el
niciodată n-a locuit...

Strânge la piept cilindrul de bambus al unei cărți
se încruntă ca un clown metafizic
și face un salt dincolo de neant.

诗人杜甫的飞跃

在风掀走茅舍的屋顶
在雨雪、饥寒、漫漫颠沛流离路
令他精疲力竭，蜷缩于自己内心之后
诗人杜甫，睁着眼睛，梦想着
将世上所有的文人，那些穷苦的
居无定所的文人
聚拢在一座大房子里。

他并不知道，愿望也会背信弃义
有时，唯有命运才能将它们实现
于是，就在返回家乡时享用了
唯一一顿丰盛的宴席后
他因消化不良，去到
另一个世界。

此刻，当我们参观那座

他从未住过的豪宅时，诗人雕像
朝我们眨了眨眼……

他双眉紧蹙，将竹简捧在胸口
恰似一名玄学小丑
突然纵身一跃，飞入虚无。

__高兴/译

Emmanuel Merle

埃曼努埃尔·迈尔勒

Né à La Mure dans les Alpes françaises en 1958. Professeur de littérature en Classes préparatoires aux Grandes Ecoles. Il écrit des poèmes et traduit de la poésie américaine. Il est le président de l'Espace Pandora à Vénissieux, une association culturelle qui promeut l'écrit et la poésie. Parmi la vingtaine d'ouvrages publiés: *Redwood, Amère Indienne, Un homme à la mer 3 recueils aux éditions Gallimard,* Pierres de folie à La Passe du Vent, Ici en exil et Dernières paroles de Perceval chez L'Escampette éditeur, Le chien de Goya et Les mots du peintre aux éditions Encre et Lumière, Le grand rassemblement chez Jacques André éditeur, Démembrements aux éditions Voix d'encre. Deux livres de traductions en français de deux poètes américains, Jennifer Barber et David Ferry.

埃曼努埃尔·迈尔勒，1958年生于阿尔卑斯山地区的拉莫尔。曾担任大学预科班的文学教师。他是“潘多拉空间”的主席。这是一家旨在推动写作和推广诗歌的文学协会。迄今已出版20余部作品。《红木》《苦涩的印第安女子》和《海上的男人》在伽利玛出版社出版。除了写诗，他还翻译美国诗歌，已出版两本译诗集。

__树才/译

Bosquet de pierres

(prier à Chengdu)

Je ne sais rien du sentiment religieux.

Seuls
le sacré de la pierre levée,
celui de la feuille errante puis tombée,
le sacré du bois dont est fait l'autel
me désignent.

A Chengdu il existe un lieu
où l'air, chargé de la puissance vibrante
des esprits, repousse le tumulte
et l'angoisse de la modernité.

Vraiment, là, comme le périmètre terrestre
d'une colonne descendue du ciel vide,

souffle le silence.

La paix des hommes.

L'odeur de l'encens est la matière d'un désir:

un lieu, un commun, un partage. Une assemblée

naturelle, un accord douloureux et fou

avec la pierre et l'arbre.

A Chengdu, dans le jardin sacré,

les pierres se lèvent,

les arbres portent des lambeaux rouges.

Baudelaire avait raison

qui voyait un lac de sang

entouré de sapins verts.

Un arbre vert et ses lanières rouges,

on dirait un être humain et ses prières.

On dirait l'espoir remplaçant les feuilles mortes.

A Chengdu, dans le jardin sacré,

les arbres et les pagodes sont du même bois,

ont la même forme,

l'extrémité des toits et des branches

se relève comme des boucles rebelles.

Les ponts couverts avec leurs galeries

d'humains assis, figurants habituels,

soudain à leur vraie place sur terre.

Ne sachant pas qu'ils ne jouent plus.

Etant là. Quoi d'autre?

A Chengdu, ce mot qui se déchire
quand on le prononce, au milieu
de ces millions d'autres moi-mêmes,
à Chengdu je trouve l'œil du cyclone,
le tourbillon figé, la respiration ultime,
le temple laïc, les petites et multiples
allées de la compassion.

石　林

（成都祷祝）

我对宗教情怀一无所知。

唯独
神圣的竖石，
恣意飞舞中缓缓飘落的叶片，
筑作祭坛的圣洁木桩
给我以启示。

在成都的一处地方，
那里的空气，
充溢着震荡颤抖的神灵的力量，
击退了现代的喧嚣与焦虑。

真的，
那里像空旷天宇间降落于尘世的一方石柱，

吹拂着静寂。
人们的安宁。

香炉的气味是心愿的介质：
一处净土，一群众生，一席分享。
一场自然集会，
一纸同石与树忧伤而疯狂的约定。

在成都，圣林中，
石块翘立，
树木则饰以朱色絮布。
波德莱尔说的有道理，
他曾看到一汪殷红的湖水
被葱郁的冷杉环抱。
一棵绿树和它的红色绣带，

人们说这是一个人同他的祷告。
人们说这是取代了枯叶的希冀。

在成都，圣林中，
树木和寺殿同一质地，
有同样的形状，
檐角同枝丫翘起
如叛逆的环。

廊桥上则绘满了闲坐的人像，
他们往往是现实生活中的配角，
却也在尘世间找到了自己的席位。
然而他们并不知道自己不是活人。
存在于成都，在那儿，这就够了，夫复何求？

在成都，

这个词被说出的那一刻，

就在千千万万个另一个我中

灰飞烟灭了。

在成都我找寻到了飓风的眼睛，

凝结的旋涡，

终极的叹息，

人间的庙宇，

各式各样饱含悲悯的林荫小径。

——丁荻/译

Freddy Ñáñez

费雷迪·楠斯

Caracas 1976. Bolivarian Republic of Venezuela. Poet, essayist and editor. As a poet he has published: *Todos los instantes, Fuego donde dice Paraíso, Bajo Palabra, El nombre de todas las cosas* and the anthology *Sombra Bajo tierra, Postal de Sequía* and *Viraje*. Recently his literary journal "Del diario hastío" has been published. He has received the following recognitions: National Prize of the book (National Center of the Book 2003 by the Anthology of the new Andean poetry The Dragoons of paper), National Prize of the Arts and the Letters (Ministery of Culture 2004 by Fuego donde dice Paraiso), International Prize of poetry Juan Beros (Direction of Culture of Tachira 2005 by Low Word), XVII Jose Antonio Ramos Sucre Poetry Biennial (Universidad de Oriente 2009 by Postal de Sequía).

费雷迪·楠斯，1976年生于委内瑞拉玻利瓦尔共和国加拉加斯，诗人、散文家和编辑。作为诗人，他发表了《所有的瞬间》《哪里说是天堂，就到哪里放火》《低调》《所有事物的名称》；选集《阴暗地下》《干旱明信片》和《转》。近期，他的文学期刊《从日记中》已经出版。他获得了以下荣誉：国家图书奖（2003年，国家图书中心，《新安第斯诗选》《龙骑兵》）、国家艺术与文学奖（2004年，文化部，《哪里说是天堂，就到哪里放火》）、胡安·贝罗斯国际诗歌奖（2005年，塔奇拉文化厅，《低调》）、第十七届何塞·安东尼奥·拉莫斯·苏克雷诗歌双年展（2009年，东方大学，《干旱明信片》）。

__费雷迪·楠斯/译

Gan Bei

Levanté el vaso y
dije tierra y la tierra
se detuvo en la sangre
para recibirme

Ella dio un paso
y en el paso
escribió su nombre:

Soy Chengdú, es decir,
el único lugar que ahora existe
el movimiento que te guarda
la lentitud donde te hospedas

Quise brindar por la distancia
pero la ciudad apuró

su noche para sanarla

y con la noche hizo la casa

y en ella hubo licor para celebrar

¡Gan bei, por los que parten!

¡Gan bei, por los que todavía no llegan!

Chengdú nos enseñó todo

Su nombre

de animal antiguo

me acompañará

fielmente

como un camino

que andan

干　杯

我举起酒杯，不禁感叹：
是这片土地！
这片土地用最热情的方式接待了我。

她踏着轻盈的步伐，
在途中写下了她的名字：
成都。

成都，好一座让你享受悠闲生活的
绝佳城市。

我曾想尽兴遥敬千杯，
无奈锦城夜晚太短暂。

但你给了我梦中的温柔乡，
让我可以在这里酣畅淋漓。

干杯，敬那些即将启程的人
干杯，敬那些将要到达这里的人。

成都向我们展示了一切。

我将永远铭记这座熊猫的故乡，
它会伴我行至远方。

__费雷迪·楠斯/译

Helmuth A. Niederle

赫尔穆特・安东・聂德乐

GEB. 1949, Lebt in Wien und Streifing/Nied-Erösterreich, Veröffentlichte zahlreiche bücher als autor, Übersetzer, Herausgeber und Kulturanthropologe. Seit 2011 ist er Präsident des österreichischen pen. Zuletzt erschienen die Gedichtsammlungen “TRAKT GERÄUMT”.

赫尔穆特·安东·聂德乐，生于1949年，现居维也纳和下奥地利州施特赖夫。他是作家、翻译家、出版人、文化人类学家，曾出版大量著作。他从2011年起担任国际笔会奥地利分会主席。他的最新一部作品是诗集《楼宇已疏散》。

__王蔚/译

Chengdu Drei Augenblicke

I Panda

Der zum Tier gewordene Spiegel der Menschen:
Pandas
fressend schlafend balgend
sich um die drängenden
    einander beim Photographieren behindernden
        glotzenden gaffenden lachenden Besucher nicht kümmernd
Tiere eben
denen die Bedeutung
die ihnen China verleiht
völlig gleichgültig ist

Das ist ein beruhigender Gegensatz
in einer Stadt
in der an allen Ecken und Enden

sich die Geschäfte in reger Betriebsamkeit ergehen

Das schwarzweiße Aussehen
verleiht den Pandas
etwas Kuscheliges
Gemahnt mich an den Teddybären
meiner Kindheit
der mich treu durch die angenommenen Abenteuer begleitete

II Der Maler

Durch das Fenster schwebt Sonnenlicht
sinkt auf weißes Papier
wandelt es in die Tiefe eines Spiegels
aus dem die Helligkeit auf das Gesicht des Malers fällt
Er beschwört in schweigender Stille

den Unwissen überwindenden

zur Weisheit verhelfenden Pinyin

Den Künstler beeindrucken

die drängenden Touristen

hemmungslos photographierend und schwatzend

nicht

Seine Pinselstriche setzt er völlig sicher

um ins Bild zu bringen

was ihm bedeutsam

Das von ihm Beschworene ist

Lichtjahre von dem entfernt

was die eiligen Besucher

als guten Schnappschuss mit nach Hause nehmen

III Die Galerie der Generäle

Siebenundvierzig Generäle aus Lehm geformt und bunt bemalt
– nicht als Ebenbilder eines Gottes –
thronen hinter Glas
als Standbilder militärischer Würde

Vor diesen Terrarien der prächtigen Erhabenheit
festgefroren in der Bewegung
tummeln sich junge Menschen
deren munteres Getuschel
die Bärte fliegen ließe
gäbe es das schützende Glas nicht

Nicht einmal einen Steinwurf entfernt
kniet eine junge Frau

vor einem Becken mit Räucherstäbchen

und bittet den Segen auf sich herab

成都三瞬

一　熊猫

作为人类镜鉴的动物：
熊猫们
进食睡觉打闹
不关心拥挤的人群
　　互相妨碍的照相者
　　　　瞪着眼睛看热闹的欢笑的游客
天生的动物
浑然不知
中国赋予它们的
意义

一种令人欣慰的悠闲
与城市对立
处处喧嚣

生意兴隆一片繁忙

黑白相间的熊猫
温暖的皮毛
依偎的怀抱
使我想起童年的
玩具熊
忠实地陪伴我度过假想的冒险生活

二　画家

阳光飘入闲窗
落在白纸上
走入镜子深处
镜子的反光照亮画家的脸
静默中他招来

克服无知

增益智慧的拼音字母

艺术家不关心

拥挤的游客

他们随意拍照

瞎聊

他自如地运笔

以形象表现

意蕴

传神

他的写意画清新淡远

远离匆促的来访者

带回家的好快照几百光年

三　武将廊

泥塑彩绘的四十七员武将
——非神像——
端坐在玻璃后面
军威之立像

玻璃柜里的崇高形象
动作已凝固
年轻人在柜前嬉戏
倘若没有防护玻璃
他们活泼的私语
就能让塑像的胡须飞起

不远处有一位
少妇

跪在香盆前

求神赐福于她

——贺骥/译

Ifor ap Glyn

艾弗・格林

Ifor ap Glyn was brought up in the Welsh speaking community in London, where his family have lived for over 130 years. He writes in Welsh, a language whose literature predates English by 700 years, and has published 5 volumes of poetry, a novel and 3 books on Welsh language and history. Ifor has won the crown for poetry twice at the National Eisteddfod, (Wales' foremost cultural gathering) and in March 2016 he was appointed Bardd Cenedlaethol Cymru/ National Poet of Wales. Promoting links with other cultures is something that has always been close to his heart and Ifor's work has been translated into a dozen languages, including Chinese.

艾弗·格林在伦敦的威尔士语社区长大。在那里，他的家族已经延续了130多年。他用威尔士语写作——威尔士语文学比英语的早700多年——出版有5部诗集、1部小说和3部关于威尔士语及其历史的书。艾弗曾两次荣获威尔士国家诗人及艺术家大会（威尔士最大且最重要的文化盛会）桂冠诗人奖。2016年3月被任命为巴德·塞内德莱索尔·西姆鲁/威尔士国家诗人。促进不同文化间联系，一直是他心中最重要的工作。其作品已被翻译成十几种语言，其中包括中文。

＿马丹/译

Mawl i Chengdu

(Dinas Du Fu)

Dyma gynefin y meistr gynt
a'i waith mor gynnil goeth
â heulwen y ddinas.

Daw'r beirdd yn barchus
i gyfarth o hyd at ryfeddod
ei belydrau cain.

Praise for Chengdu

(City of Du Fu)

This was home to the master once,
his work as fine and concise
as city sunshine.

Today's appreciative poets
still bark in marvel
at its elegant rays.

(Translation from Welsh original)

成都颂

（杜甫之乡）

此地曾是诗圣故里，
他的诗凝练有力
如城中日光。

今日诗人慕名向往
仍然在啧啧称赞
这文雅之光。

—马丹/译

时间深处的城市

Igor Costanzo

伊戈・科斯坦佐

Igor Costanzo (1980-) is an Italian poet and writer. He graduated in Verona in Modern Literature and Modern Philology. He currently teaches at Brescia. He was assistant to Francesco Conz but its cultural promotion activities continues, founded the publishing Volo Press, publishing and translating some volumes of Paul Polansky and Enrico Ghedi first, then directing with Beppe Costa and Stefania Battistella necklace "Unpublished rare and different" the Seam Editions. Igor Costanzo devotes his entire life to poetry, meeting poets such as, among others, Jack Hirman, Hermann Nitsch, Lawrence Ferlinghetti; as chairman of the culture of the town of Moniga del Garda (Italy), organizes numerous meetings poetic and cultural bringing in Italy several important personalities, from the world of literature. In 2013 he was the promoter of the lifetime achievement award given to Fernando Arrabal to Moniga.

伊戈·科斯坦佐（1980— ），意大利诗人、作家。曾于维罗纳市攻读现代文学和现代哲学专业。目前任教于布雷西亚市。他曾担任弗朗西斯科·贡兹的助理，继而独立从事文化传播活动，创立沃洛出版社，最初翻译和出版保罗·波兰斯基和恩里科·戈蒂的诗集，后来与贝普科斯塔和斯特法尼亚·巴蒂斯特拉共同策划“未出版的、罕见的和与众不同的”系列。伊戈将其所有的精力都投入诗歌领域，与众多诗人接触，如杰克·赫曼、赫尔曼·尼奇、劳伦斯·费林奇等。作为意大利加达湖上的莫尼加镇的文化主席，他组织了无数的诗歌和文学活动，将世界文学界的重量级人物邀请到意大利。2013年，在他的提议下，费尔南多·阿拉巴尔在莫尼加接受了终身成就奖。

__梅申友/译

Sotto le stelle di Chengdu

La cerimonia del te
ci accoglie
nella casa di Li Bai
se ne sente ancora l'odore
della sua grappa di riso
e mi misuro con l'uomo
l'unico uomo
che ha abbracciato
la luna per intero
portandola con sé
nell'abisso

immensità
quando la notte mi avvolge
in questa allegra follia
ospitalità infinita dell'ultimo

luogo sulla terra che prende
la parola ancora sul serio

ma manchi solo tu
con me
sotto le stelle
di Chengdu
L'ospite va accolto
con calma
va preso per mano
porta storie di un paese
lontano
come il Gran Khan
con Marco Polo
l'ospite allieta la notte
la splendida notte

in cui manchi solo tu

con me

sotto le stelle

di Chengdu

La mia partenza

bagnata di lacrime

le pure lacrime delle fanciulle

acqua e sapone

di panni lavati al fiume

quando passa la febbre

che ti riporta dopo un lungo

viaggio a tenere ancora in pugno

questa terra unica di Chengdu

dove manchi solo tu

在成都的星空下

李白故居
用品茶的仪式
来迎接我们
那里的米酒
馨香犹存
我与一个男人的对决
唯一的男人
他曾敞开胸怀
拥抱月亮
并且带着它
共赴深渊

广袤无垠
当深夜将我笼罩
在这快乐的疯狂
极致的好客

在世间最后的土地
这里仍旧将话语当真

唯独少了一个你
与我一起
在成都的
星空之下
待客之道
须平静地
握着他的手
带着一个国家的历史
如此遥远
就像忽必烈汗
接待马可·波罗
这愉快的客人，深夜
在灿烂的深夜
唯独少了一个你

与我一起
在成都的
星空之下

我的离去
泪水浸润了眼睛
少女纯洁的泪水
水与肥皂
河流中清洗的衣衫
一次遥远的旅行之后
当热潮退去
仍旧握在手中的
是成都这片独一无二的土地
唯独少了一个你

__魏怡/译

Jami Proctor Xu

徐贞敏

Jami Proctor Xu is a poet, translator, and mother who writes in English and Chinese. Her Chinese poetry collections include *Shimmers* (2013), and *Suddenly Starting to Dance* (2016). Her English chapbook, *Hummingbird Ignites a Star*, was published in 2014. Her poems appear in journals and anthologies in China, India, and the US, and have been translated into Vietnamese, Bengali, and Spanish. Jami has translated collections of Chinese poets Jidi Majia and Song Lin, and she is translating a collection of poems by Zhai Yongming. She is a recipient of a 2013 Zhujiang Poetry Award.

徐贞敏，美国人，女，诗人、翻译家，一位用中英双语写作的母亲。其中文诗集有《轻轻的闪光》（2013）、《突然起舞》（2016），英文诗集有《蜂鸟点燃了一颗星星》（2014）。她的诗出现在中国、美国、印度等国家的刊物和诗选中，也已经被翻译成越南语、孟加拉语、西班牙语。她翻译过吉狄马加和宋琳的诗集，目前正在翻译翟永明的诗集。2013年，获珠江诗歌节旅华诗歌奖。

__徐贞敏、王蔚/译

Chengdu, Chengdu

I can honestly say if it weren't for Chengdu, it's likely I wouldn't be a poet, or at least not a bilingual poet. Sure, I would have written poetry and given it to friends, but I probably wouldn't have ever made the decision to start publishing my work, be a poet out in the world, and begin writing in Chinese. When I was growing up in Arizona, my schools didn't really include much poetry in the curriculum. Sure, in high school, we read many of the well-known American poets, but most of the poets we read had all died before I was born. My schools didn't invite any poets to come read to us or talk to us about being a poet, so even though I'd written poetry as a child, won a poetry contest in high school, and imagined myself becoming a writer, that idea/dream felt very distant from my lived reality, and I ended up going to a graduate school and decided I would pursue a more typical life-path and become a teacher and scholar. I suppose I would have eventually started sending my poems out to be published, but it might have taken more than half my life if it hadn't been for a trip I made to Chengdu in 2001.

At the time I was doing a PhD in Chinese Literature and doing research on contemporary Chinese poetry, so my advisor, Lydia Liu, suggested I come to Chengdu to meet with Zhai Yongming and to visit her bar, White Nights, where local poets and artists hung out. Before that, I had known Chengdu had a long history as a place where poetry flourished—I had visited Xue Tao's statue at Wangjianglou the first time I came to Chengdu in 1994, and I had read Du Fu's work and visited Du Fu's thatched cottage—but I didn't know that Chengdu's place as a center of poetry and art had continued to the present. I had visited Chengdu in 1994 and 1995, and had fallen in love with Chengdu's old wooden buildings, the slow pace of life, the teahouses along the riverbank where people sat, drinking tea, playing cards and Majiang, and eating melon seeds. I ate hot pot and went to Sichuan opera, and knew this was a city I would return to many times, so when Lydia suggested I come to Chengdu to meet

Zhai Yongming, Zhai and I hit it off right away, and she offered to introduce me to several local poets. The first night we went to a bar owned by another poet—where I first met Yang Li, Xiao An, Liu Tao, and several other local poets. The next afternoon I went to Zhai's bar, White Nights, in its original location in the Yulin district. She introduced me to the poet, Tang Danhong, and we sat and talked for three hours straight before she, Zhai, and some Beijing musicians who were in town all piled into Danhong Jeep to ride to a small town outside of Chengdu. Two rivers merge there, and we arrived in the evening right as the sun was setting. They rented a wooden boat and ordered dinner, and we all spent the next six or so hours talking, eating, drinking, laughing, and quoting poetry while floating on the wooden boat under a full moon. People quoted Li Bai and spoke of him chasing the moon's reflection in the water. I remember feeling like I'd found a place and people with whom I felt totally at ease.

Later, Zhai, Danhong, and several other Chinese poet friends encouraged me to send my poems out for publication. Back then I was only writing in English, but once I told Zhai a dream I had and she said, "You're a poet. Just write that dream down and it's already a poem." Later, she and other Chinese poet friends encouraged me to begin writing in Chinese. I moved to Beijing in 2008 and began going to Chengdu whenever I could—mostly to attend poetry and art events at White Nights, but later I also began spending more time with Chengdu's artists and drawing inspiration from the work of and interactions with the painter He Duoling, his students like Wu Jiangtao, as well as the sculptor Zhu Cheng, the architect Liu Jiakun, and poets like Jimu Langge, He Xiaozhu, Li Yawei, and others. One reason Chengdu is a paradise for poets is its rich community of artists, writers, scholars, musicians, students, and community members who exchange work and ideas. Much of this comes about in the playful, fun conversations so typical in Chengdu, where ideas and jokes fly, collide, and soon become art installations, books of essays, or poems. Or, when you dance at Night Whites and suddenly a poem begins taking shape inside you. What makes Chengdu a city of poetry isn't any of its high-rises, widened roads, or its increasingly global character. Chengdu is a city of poetry because of its rich tradition of poetry and art; the persistent insistence on making days meaningful here—by spending time with friends, eating, talking, laughing, creating—the generosity between writers, artists, musicians, and the community of readers, the energy and life of the city, the long hot pot dinners and midnight barbecues, and the fact that there is support for poetry and the arts here, in the form of festivals, readings, talks, art exhibits, and community events. When I tell people that Chengdu is my heaven, these are the reasons why.

成都，成都

老实说，如果不是成都的缘故，我可能不会成为一个诗人，或者说至少不会成为一个双语诗人。当然，我会写一些诗送给朋友，但是我也许永远都不会决定去出版我的作品，成为一个为人所知的诗人，并且尝试用中文写作。在我成长的亚利桑那州母校的课堂上并没有真正太多与诗歌相关的内容。当然，我在高中时代曾拜读过许多赫赫有名的美国诗人的作品，但他们大都在我出生之前就已经驾鹤西去了。我们学校没有邀请任何诗人来为我们朗读诗歌或者举办关于如何成为诗人的讲座，尽管如此，我还是从小写诗。高中时期，我在一个诗歌比赛中崭露头角，幻想着有朝一日成为一名作家，虽然这样的念头或者梦想离我所处的现实相去甚远。最后，我上了研究生院并且下定决心要走一条更普通的人生道路，去成为一名老师和学者。虽然，我想总有一天我会将我的诗付梓出版，但要不是因为2001年的成都之行，那一天可能会迟到半辈子。

彼时，我还在攻读中国文学的博士学位，从事中文现代诗的研究，我的导师莉迪亚·刘建议我到成都见一见翟永明，去她的“白夜”酒馆坐坐，那里是当地诗人和艺术家的聚会之所。在那之前，我就知道成都是一个历史悠久的诗歌之城——1994年，我第一次踏足成都的时候，曾去拜谒过望江楼的薛涛像，在拜读杜甫的作品之后又慕名去了杜甫草堂——可我却不知道成都至今都还是诗与艺术的中心。我在1994年和1995年都到过成都，那时我就迷上了成都的木结构建筑和怡然自得的慢生活，还有那河边的茶馆。人们安坐品茶，打打纸牌，搓搓麻将，嗑嗑瓜子。当我吃过了火锅，看过了川剧，我就知道我与这座城市结下了不解之缘。而莉迪亚就建议我来成都见翟永明。当时，我与翟一拍即合，她还向我引荐了一些当地诗人。当晚，我们去了另一间诗人开的酒馆。在那里，我遇见了杨黎、小安、刘涛和其他一些当地诗人。翌日午后，我又去了翟永明在玉林区旧址的“白夜”酒馆。她将我引荐给诗人唐丹鸿，我们畅谈了三个钟头。后来，我同翟以及一些从北京远道而来的音乐家们挤进了丹鸿的吉普车，一道去往成都郊外的一个小镇。那里两江交汇。我们恰好在日薄西山之时抵达了目的地。他们租了一艘木船，点好了晚餐。在接下来的六个多小时里，我们在月下泛舟湖上，谈笑风生，吟诗作对。有人还引李白诗，谈到他水中捞月的传说。我记得那种感觉就像找到了归宿，与他们相伴我感到无比自在。

之后，翟、丹鸿和其他一些中国诗人朋友鼓励我将我的诗作付梓。那时我还只是用英文写作，但当我将曾经的梦想告诉翟的时候，她对我说："你是个诗人。将梦想写下来本身就已经是一首诗了。"自那以后，她和其他的中国诗人朋友都鼓励我尝试用中文创作。2008年，我移居北京。一有机会，我便会去成都——主要是参加一些在"白夜"举办的诗歌与艺术活动。后来，我开始花更多时间与成都的艺术家们往来，从他们的作品里汲取灵感，并和他们切磋交流，比如与画家何多苓，以及他的学生们，包括吴江涛，又如与雕塑家朱成、建筑设计师刘家琨，还有诸如吉木狼格、何小竹、李亚伟等诗人。成都作为诗歌天堂的一个原因就在于它有着囊括了大量作家、学者、音乐家和学生的社区，而这些社区成员们都互相交流作品和思想。趣味横生的交谈在成都已经司空见惯，在这里，想法和玩笑能不时迸发，彼此碰撞，须臾之间就成了装饰艺术、妙笔丹青。又或者当你在“白夜”跳舞的时候，顷刻间，诗作便已成竹在胸。使成都成为诗歌之城的，并不是它的摩天高楼、宽广的道路，也不是它日益提升的国际形象。成都之所以作为诗歌之城，是因为富饶的诗与艺术的传统，是因为在这里，每一天都被赋予意义（通过与朋友共度时光、分享创作、谈笑风生），是因为作家、音乐家以及读者社区之间的包容，是因为这座城的活力，耗时甚长的火锅晚餐与午夜烧烤，以及这里用节日、读书会、沙龙、艺术展与社区活动等形式对诗歌与艺术的支持。若我逢人便诉说成都是我的天堂，那以上种种就是原因所在。

__徐贞敏、王蔚/译

时间深处的城市

Jüri Talvet

尤里・塔尔维特

Born in 1945 in Pärnu, Estonia, received his Ph.D degree in Western literatures from Leningrad / Saint Petersburg University (1981). Since 1992 he is Chair Professor at Tartu University. After his poetic debut book *Awakenings* (1981), he has published nine books of poetry in Estonian, of which book-long selections have appeared in English, French, Spanish, Italian, Romanian and Catalan. Also his essays have been published in English, Spanish, Catalan and Italian. He has been awarded a number of prizes and distinctions, in 2016 he was elected as Member of Academia Europaea.

尤里·塔尔维特，1945年生于爱沙尼亚帕尔努，1981年从圣彼得堡国立大学（列宁格勒国立大学）获得西方文学博士学位。自1992年起，他开始在塔尔图大学任职讲席教授。继开山诗集《觉醒》（1981）试水文坛，他不久又创作了九部母语诗集，其间还出版了英语、法语、西班牙语、意大利语、罗马尼亚语、加泰罗尼亚语的译本。同时他的散文也出版了英语、西班牙语、加泰罗尼亚语和意大利语的译本。他笔耕不辍，屡获殊荣，在2016年又被推选为欧洲科学院的成员。

__刘泽/译

Chengdus kohtasin Laozid

Tean et see oli tema
Tean niisama kindlalt
  nagu tunnen iseennast
  (või ei tunne)

Chengdus oli tal oma elamine
(reservaat, võiks öelda)
Ta istus klaasmajakeses
  keset bambusejupikeste kuhja
  näsis mõnd õrnemat võrset
  rohkem tundis ja mõtles kui sõi

Ümberringi laskus vaikset
uduvihma bambuselehtedele
mis on ühtlaselt-hellalt voolitud
ujedad-ilusad hiina tüdrukud

Niipea kui ta märkas rahvahulka
peitunud olgu mineviku või tuleviku
sõjardeid või nuhke
nende kavalat haukumist kuuldes
puges ta oma rohelise maja
kaugeimasse tihnikunurka

Ta ütleb et bambuselehtedes
tundis ta ära Ilusa Naise –
iga rahva lunastuse
iginoore lootuse

Jah see on tema
Tundsin ta ära ses noores
bambuselehes
kes õpib prantsuse keelt

ja kelle huuli

ühegi mehe huuled

puutunud iial ei ole

Kelle pruunjast palest

voolab üle tõmmum õhetus

kui ta mult küsib:

Kuidas on sinu rahva keeles

"Mis su nimi on?"

In Chengdu I met Lao-tzu

I know it was him
I know it as surely
  as I know myself
  (or don't know myself)

In Chengdu he had his own place
(a reservation, one might say)
He sat in his bamboo-strewn glass room
  He nibbled on tender shoots
  He was engaged in feeling
  and meditating, more than in eating

Around him a silent mist
fell on bamboo leaves
that are flawlessly-lovingly formed
shy-lovely Chinese girls

As soon as he noticed a past or future
warrior or spy
lurking in the crowd
cleverly barking
he slunk to the farthest, most thicketed
corner of his green house

He says in the bamboo leaves
he sensed the Beautiful Woman –
every nation's perpetual
hope for redemption

Yes I know it was him
I felt him in that young
bamboo leaf that studies French
and whose lips

have never been touched

by a man's kiss

A darker glow runs over

her brownish face

when she asks me:

How is it in your language

"What is your name?"

(Translated by Jüri Talvet and H. L. Hix)

在成都我遇见老子

我认出那是他
我确实认出了他
　　就像我认识我自己
　　（或不认识我自己）

在成都他有自己的住处
（专用的，有人说）
他坐在遍植翠竹的玻璃房里
　　小口地咬着嫩芽
　　他专注于感受
　　和沉思，甚于嚼食

在他周围，安静的雾
落到竹叶上
竹叶完美成形于娇羞迷人的
中国少女之手

一旦察觉过去或未来的
武士或间谍
潜伏在人群中
他就机警地叫喊
退到离温室最远
灌木丛最密集的角落

他在竹叶中说话
他感受美丽的女人——
每个民族救赎的
永恒希望

是的，我认出那是他
我在青青竹叶间
感受他，吟咏法语的竹叶
其嘴唇

从未被男人

吻过

一道更隐秘的红光涌过

她褐色的面颊

这时她问我：

用你的语言怎么说

“你叫什么名字？”

__程一身/译

时／间／深／处／的／城／市

Krisztina Tóth

克里斯蒂娜·托斯

She is one of the most highly acclaimed Hungarian poets. She is the winner of several awards, including the Graves Prize (1996), Déry Tibor Prize (1996), József Attila Prize (2000) and her poetry ad prose has been translated into many languages. Since her first collection of short stories was published in 2006, she is listed amongst the best contemporary writers of Central Europe. Krisztina Tóth lives in Budapest, where apart from writing and translating poetry, she designs and produces stained glass windows. She was recently awarded the Laureate Prize, one of the the highest recognition in Hungarian literature.

克里斯蒂娜·托斯是匈牙利最著名的诗人之一。曾获得多个奖项，包括1996年的“格雷福斯奖”、1996年的“提波尔·戴瑞奖”、2000年的“阿提拉·约瑟夫奖”。其诗歌和散文作品被翻译成多国语言。2006年，她的第一部短篇小说集发表后，她便跻身中欧地区最优秀的现当代作家行列。如今，克里斯蒂娜·托斯住在布达佩斯，每天除了写作与翻译诗歌，她还喜欢自己设计和制作彩色玻璃窗。最近，她还获得了桂冠奖，成为匈牙利文学史上获得荣誉最高的作家之一。

—王蔚/译

Éjszakai eső

Gyerekkoromban
aszfaltkrétával írtam az útra.
Azt hittem, látni lehet majd
az űrből is azt a mondatot.

Aztán néztük a tizedikről
az esőt. Nem baj - mondta a Móni
legközelebb majd
odafestjük a szavakat.

Eltelt azóta negyven év
Móni meghalt, én egy idegen
földrész idegen városában
nézem a felhőkarcolókat.

Pandák élnek errefelé: ha elmesélném

Móninak, el se hinné.

Hát ott vagy, mosolyogna odaátról, és

a pandákra is csak annyit

felelne, hogy világ mégsem

csak fekete-fehér.

Elfelejtettem, mit akartam

üzenni akkor. Már csak a

zápor szeretnék lenni.

Az az egykori, abban

a régi pillanatban, ahogy a betonra

ér, és színesen visszafröccsen.

夜　雨

小时候
我用粉笔在路上写字。
我以为，从太空
也能看见我写的那句话。

后来，我们从十楼
看雨。没关系——莫尼说
下次我们再把
词画上。

四十年过去了
莫尼死了，我在一片陌生
大陆的陌生城市里
望着摩天大楼。

熊猫就住在这儿：我若是跟莫尼

这么说，他一定不信。

你就在那儿，他面对着我微笑

关于熊猫，他

只能说，世界也不

只有黑与白。

我忘了，那时

我想表达什么。我只想

成为一场暴雨。

那是曾经的

旧时光里，当它拍击到

水泥地面时，又心甘情愿地飞溅回来。

__舒苏乐/译

Mohammed El Amraoui

穆罕默德・艾拉・阿姆哈维

Poète, performeur et traducteur, né en 1964 au Maroc, vit en France depuis 1989. Etudes de linguistique et de philosophie. Ecrit en français et en arabe. Se produit dans différents lieux et festivals, seul ou avec des musiciens en France et à l'étranger. Traduit en plusieurs langues. Dernières publications: Des moineaux dans la tête, éd. Jacques André, 2016; Ex., éd. Fidel Anthelme X, 2013; Accouchement de choses, éd. Dumerchez, 2008; Récits, partitions et photographies, éd. La Passe du Vent, 2007; La fenêtre, dimanche et autres jours (en arabe), éd. Fadâ'ât, Amman, 2007; De ce côté-ci et alentour, éd. L'Idée bleue, 2006. A traduit plusieurs livres parmi lesquelles: Anthologie de la poésie marocaine contemporaine, Maison de la Poésie Rhône-Alpes, 2006.

穆罕默德·艾拉·阿姆哈维，诗人、翻译家、诗歌行为艺术家。1964年生于摩洛哥的古城菲斯。1989年移居法国。攻读语言和哲学专业。用法语和阿拉伯语写作。在法国和其他国家参加过诗歌节。其作品被译成多种语言。出版诗集有《头脑中的麻雀》《事物的分娩》《这边和周围》等。2006年翻译了《摩洛哥当代诗选》。

__树才/译

Chengdu

Dans une petite cour de la vieille rue Jinli
une jeune femme assise, dos bien
droit,
joue au qanun un air ancien,
une robe bleue-blanche soyeuse à traîne où
miroite la broderie de Shu
un visage lisse où
se figent les heures
les yeux baissés ignorent
les silhouettes autour qui
déambulent, s'arrêtent puis
repartent timidement comme pour
s'excuser d'avoir foulé un espace
frêle, incompatible avec
le dehors
bruyant brouillon

Seuls les doigts tissent, attachent,
détachent, piquent
Et les notes réitérées comme
vaguelettes
se retournent sur elles-mêmes

Dans l'interstice des notes,
précaire, essentiel,
l'instant se découpe d'un seul coup,
frontière entre sommeil et éveil
et crevasse où
l'on rêve par petits bouts,
on ferme, on ouvre, en douceur, mécaniquement presque,
on se laisse se diluer,
on laisse diluer,
on dilue

le jour,

on le dilue

dans une nuit soudaine,

appropriée,

on ne veut plus,

plus savoir

où l'on est,

on laisse tirer,

s'échouer dans le vrai,

le reste peu importe,

et j'y arrive enfin

Combien de temps

suis-je resté

là,

je ne sais plus mais

peu

de temps

Je me suis rappelé un vers de Du

Fu:

La lune semble bouillonner, le

grand fleuve coule.

J'ai regardé l'heure. Il était 23 h

23

(je n'avais pas encore changé l'heure

sur ma montre)

La nuit

d'ailleurs

est venue

s'incruster

dans

le jour

d'ici

Les notes s'éloignent,

les pas aussi

S'éloigner dans les notes, me dis-je,

levant les yeux vers

les immeubles

innombrables qui

cognent la grisaille

et se concurrencent en taille et noirceur

et blancheur

Des vêtements pendent aux balcons, pendent

Et

la lumière s'incline

en douceur

avant que les lumières des enseignes

fractionnent l'espace

en espaces

globuleux phosphorescents

s'enduisant

d'une brume irréelle

avec noir dedans

et autour.

Idéogrammes luisants et une petite

rumeur s'approche -

des langues s'enchevêtrent -

inflexions des voix, de l'âme et du

sens. Je respire les parties et le tout.

Les amis ne sont pas loin.

成　都

在锦里老街上有一方小小的庭院，
一个女孩坐着，
背挺得直立立，
在卡农琴上弹奏着一首古老的乐曲，
蓝白相间的丝裙拖着地
刺在上面的蜀绣闪着光
光滑的面庞
凝住了时光
低眉的眼眸忽略了四周闲逛的身影，
人们驻足片刻然后又悄然离去，
仿佛在为践踏了一隅轻柔而致歉，
这里同外界
嘈杂的喧嚣
格格不入
唯独指尖在编织，碰触，
抽离，断奏

而悠悠琴鸣恰如
圈圈涟漪
百转千回

在音符的间隙，
不期而必然的空白
顷刻的无声一下有了轮廓，
这是睡梦与苏醒的交界
在时空隙缝里
我们一点一点地幻想，
我们蜷缩，我们敞怀，悠然地，趋近于无意识，
我们恣意消融，
我们任它消融，
我们消融
那一日，
我们把它消融，

在一个突如其来的夜，
一切刚刚好，
我们不再想，
不再想知道
我们身处何方，
我们任凭牵曳，
在真实境域里停息，
其余都无关紧要了，
而我最终抵达那里

究竟有多久
我停留在那里，
我不会知道，但
零星
片刻

我回想起杜甫的一句诗：

月涌大江流。

我看了看表。23点。

23

（我还没来得及调手表上的时间）

别处的

夜晚

嵌入

这里的

白日

乐声飘远了，

脚步声同样在琴鸣里渐逝，

我自言自语，

我抬起眼睛

望向数不清的楼宇

它们

敲击着灰蒙蒙的云天

鳞次栉比，黑白相交，

衣服则挂在阳台，垂吊着

天光呢，

温柔地弯着腰

随后，

店家招牌上的光线

把空间分割成了

生辉的团块

上面涂抹着

一缕虚幻的薄雾

内里发黑

轮廓也如此。

文字嵌着光

一点点喧闹正在靠近

言语夹杂其中

混合着变幻的声音、灵魂以及语义。

我呼吸着这部分以及全部。

朋友们就在不远处。

__丁获/译

Moon, Chung-hee

文贞姬

Moon, Chung-hee is one of the most celebrated poets living in South Korea today. She was born in 1947 in the southern part of the Korean Peninsula and was raised in Seoul. Moon has published numerous books of poetry, some of which are: *I Am Moon*, and *The Sea of Karma*. Moon is a recipient of numerous prestigious Korean and international literary prizes, most notably the Cikada Prize, the Swedish literary award founded for East Asian poets, in 2010. A participant in the Iowa International Writers' Program in 1995, she served as the President of the Society of Korean Poets from 2015 to 2016. Moon is currently an endowed professor of poetry at the Department of Creative Writing, Dongguk University in Seoul, Korea.

文贞姬，当今韩国最著名的诗人之一。她于1947年出生于朝鲜半岛南部，在首尔长大。她出版了许多诗集，如《我是月亮》《噶玛之海》。她曾获得韩国和其他国家的许多文学奖项。最著名的是2010年获得的斯卡达奖，这是为东亚诗人创立的瑞典文学奖。在1995年爱荷华国际作家计划的参与者中，她担任2015—2016年的韩国诗人协会会长。她目前被聘为韩国首尔东古大学诗歌创意写作系教授。

__薛舟/译

보초당에서

이 정원을 전생에 거닌 적이 있었던 것 같다.
두보 초당에 들어서자
숲속에 잠겨있던 고요가
일제히 환호하며 나를 반가워했다.

바람이 내 머리칼을 쓰다듬었다.
걱정마라! 잠시 지나가는 시대의 바람들
때로 사납지만
적정마라! 고달픈 삶
곧 부드러워 지리라
맑은 시가 되어
사람을 더욱 풍요롭게 해줄 것이다.

이 정원을 전생에 거닌 적이 있었던 것 같다
포근한 저녁이 내려오는 시간
향기로운 숲에 서있는 검은 비석에서

시인의 절창이 반짝인다

기억과 상처로

깊은 천년 시인의 꿈이

한 마리 나비 처럼 날아오른다.

杜甫草堂

前生好像来过这庭院。
刚刚步入杜甫草堂
潜藏在树林中的寂静
齐声欢呼，迎接我的到来。

风抚摸我的发丝。
别担心！不时经过的时代的风
偶尔有些猛烈
别担心！苦痛的生活
很快就会变得柔软
变成明亮的诗
让人们的生活更加丰饶。

前世好像来过这庭院。
温暖的黄昏落幕时
矗立在芬芳树林里的黑色石碑上

闪烁着诗人的绝唱。

诗人千年的梦

因回忆和伤痛而深邃

宛如一只蝴蝶翩翩起舞。

—薛舟/译

챙두의 보석

비행기로 불과 몇 시간,
어쩌면 고향보다 가까운 챙두이다.
젊은 미래의 시인이
판다와 함께 나를 반기었다.
7년만인가?
기억속의 챙두는 보이지 않고
그 사이 하늘을 치솟는 문명이
꽃처럼 피어나
내 앞을 가로 막는다.
강물처럼 흘러가는 자동차들의 물결이
은비늘 달린 물고기들처럼 풍요롭다.
보석처럼 깊은 시혼을 품고 있는 도시
세계에서 온 시인들이
천년의 시혼에다 고달픈 발을 담갔다.
서로 다른 고독과 고통을

사랑을 속삭이듯

서로에게 시로 읊어주었다.

成都的宝石

乘飞机去成都只要几小时
或许比故乡更近。
年轻的未来诗人
和熊猫一起迎接我。
有七年了吧?
记忆中的成都不见了
直刺苍穹的文明
如花绽放
挡在我的面前。
车流如江水流动
又像长满银鳞的鱼。
这是有着宝石般深邃诗魂的城市。
来自全世界的诗人们
脚踩千年的诗魂
用诗吟诵

各不相同的孤独和痛苦
好像说着情话。

——薛舟/译

Paola Pigani

帕拉·毕佳妮

Née en France de parents Italiens émigrés en Charente dans les années soixante, Paola Pigani est poète, nouvelliste et romancière. Inspirée par le monde rural de ses origines, elle aime aussi écrire sur la ville, l'exil, le déracinement, la photographie et la peinture. Elle a participé à diverses anthologies. Son premier roman N'entre pas dans mon âme avec tes chaussures publié aux éditions Liana Levi en 2013 a été récompensé par de nombreux prix et traduit en finnois en 2017. Son second roman Venus d'ailleurs est paru en 2015.

帕拉·毕佳妮，法国诗人、小说家。父母均为意大利移民。现居里昂。2013年出版的第一部小说《别穿着鞋踏进我的灵魂》，被译成英语等多种外国语言，获得数个奖项。她从故乡的农村世界汲取灵感，写作主题涉及城乡、流亡、失根、摄影和绘画。她的第二部小说《来自别处》于2015年出版。

_树才/译

Chengdu

Chengdu étend sur nous

La douceur d'un ciel gris

Le fleuve Modi ses calligraphies

D'eaux languides

Où deux cygnes noirs

Suivent un chemin invisible

Le jardin de Dù Fǔ

Est planté de beautés orphelines

Buvons encore un peu

De ce vin translucide

Partageons notre ivresse

Avec les poètes

Nous pousserons la porte du temple Wenshu

Marcherons jusqu' où tombent d'un arbre seul

Des prières en filaments rouges

Jusqu'où le temps nous parlera

D'une ville électrique et suave

Aux voix humaines se mêleront des joies d'oiseaux

Dans le ciel de Chengdu

成 都

成都舒展于我们之上
温柔的灰色天宇
磨底河
懒洋洋的河水
两只黑天鹅
追随着一条隐形细流

杜甫草堂
栽植着孤芳野草
我们依旧啜饮着
半透明的酒
和诗人们
同享沉醉

我们将轻启文殊院的殿门
直至那孤树偃卧

红带垂落的栖身之处

直到时间告知我们

一座生动怡人的城市

人声中裹挟着群鸟的欣悦

在成都的天空中

__丁荻/译

Salvador Medina Barahona

萨尔瓦多·梅迪纳·巴拉霍纳

Nacido en Panamá en 1973, es un poeta con varios roles. Se han publicado un total de seis poemas, incluido *The Days I Have Been*, que ganó el Premio Nacional de Literatura Ricardo Miró, el galardón más prestigioso en el mundo literario panameño. Otros premios que se han ganado incluyen el Premio Rohello Sinan de Literatura Centroamericana (2001-2002), Stella Citila National Poetry Award (2000). Hoy es profesor en el Departamento de Poesía de la Universidad Panameña de Ciencia y Tecnología y docente en el Instituto Nacional de Cultura.

萨尔瓦多·梅迪纳·巴拉霍纳，1973年出生于巴拿马，是一位身兼数职的诗人。他一共出版了6本诗集，其中《我走过的日子》获得了里卡多·米罗国家文学奖。该奖项是巴拿马文学界最具权威的奖项。他曾获得的其他奖项有罗赫略·思南中美洲文学奖（2001—2002）、斯特拉·西铁拉国家诗歌奖（2000）。现在，他是巴拿马科技大学诗歌系的教师，同时也是国家文化学院的教师。

__王敏/译

Chengdu

De estos lugares no se libra nadie,
como una ola no se libra de romper en la piedra
que vulnera su impacto
o en el litoral de una infancia
tan antigua como el miedo.

Son fundados estos lugares por la Poesía
para que el poeta,
ese peregrino de luces pardas y oquedades
encendidas, los pueble,
con humanidad y asombro, y los funde,
otra vez,
con su aventura,
su palabra.

Chengdu es uno de esos sitios que animan

la vocación del regreso.
Pocos podrían olvidar sus calles
de frutas llenas, y
vegetales tan extraños y coloridos
que habría que llevar gafas de sol
para no enceguecer.

Sus monasterios, costras de un pasado
que aún nos quema, siguen
buscando una verdad que allí,
como en todas partes,
se oculta.

Por si existiera la cifra terrible del olvido,
habríamos de inventar una tregua de sueños
para recordarnos en sus callejas

o grandes avenidas ataviadas de árboles
y otros verdes que si nombro mueren.

Pero si un poeta, forjador de sueños,
domador de pesadillas, ha viajado
por encima de los mares,
oteado entre las nubes el inmenso
y desolado paisaje de Groenlandia,
presentido las luciérnagas
de una Mongolia a punto de despertar;
oído, en fin, el pálpito de una ballena blanca
en las alas del gran pájaro de acero,
es porque algo debe decir.

(No se cruzan grandes distancias
para recibir homenajes y callar.)

No viaja tantas horas un poeta para guardar silencio.
Para ser celebrado por las cámaras de televisión.
Perseguido por los ágiles fotógrafos.
Comentado amablemente por los diarios
de la gran ciudad a la que ha asistido
como a una especie de convención de mudos.

El poeta viaja con su palabra.
Y para decir su palabra viaja.
Sin que le teman. Para volcarse en su oficio...
Sí, está bien, debajo de los reflectores,
aunque también fuera de ellos.
Frente a los ojos de la gente.
Cerca de sus oídos.
Cerca.

El poeta viaja para ser,
estar, hablar, ¿ya dije hablar?,
perderse entre las multitudes,
hacerse agua luminosa
en los ríos coagulados de la niebla.

Viaja para romper el silencio
que a diario lo atenaza en su casa.
Viaja a una nueva casa
para saber que tiene voz.
Viaja para decir,
sin que nadie tema a lo que dice.

Sí. Chengdu es uno de esos sitios que animan
la vocación del regreso. Es una casa lejos de casa.

Y todo conspira para volver.

Y tanta belleza nos llama en espirales.

Y tanta voz. Tantos oídos. Tanto diálogo pendiente en la voz.

Chengdu, ah, Chengdu, escúchame!

成　都

谁都离不开这些地方，
就像波浪一样
不是撞击岩石
就是消失在童年
像恐惧一样古老的海岸上。

这些地方的创建是为了诗歌
诗人是棕色光明
和被点燃洞穴的朝圣者，
为了在此繁衍，他们
带着惊喜和人文情怀
将这样的地方创建，
用他们的奇遇，
用他们的语言。

成都就是这样的地方

它会激起人们重游的志向。
人们忘不了它的街巷
到处是水果，
和如此奇异、多彩的植物
天空如此晴朗
人们必须戴墨镜遮阳。

它的庙宇，过去留下的外壳
依然使我们感到滚烫，
依然在寻求真理
真理在那里
如同在各地隐藏。

倘若真的有忘却的可怕的密码
我们要想方设法停止梦想
以便回忆成都的街巷

宽阔的林荫大道
以及其他的绿色——
我要叫得出名字，它们会死亡。

然而如果一个诗人，
美梦的锻造者，噩梦的驯服者，
漂洋过海而来，从云间
俯瞰茫茫寰宇
和格陵兰的荒凉，
预感到即将
醒来的蒙古国的点点荧光；
最终，在钢铁巨鸟的翅膀
听到一条白鲸的震荡，
那是因为他有话要讲。
（穿过遥远的距离，不是
为了接受敬意和沉默不语）

诗人长途旅行不是为了保持寂静。
不是为了电视台的摄影。
不是为了机敏摄影师的追踪。
不是为了得到这座大城市
各家报刊亲切的述评
他来这里参加活动
并非聋哑人签署的协定。

诗人带着他的话语出行。
出行为了发声。
这是它的指责。不会令人惊恐。
是的，好，在聚光灯下，
哪怕照不到他。
面对人们的眼睛。
让他们倾听。
倾听。

诗人出行是为了存在，
出现，发声，我说过发声了吗？
为了融入人群，
化作闪光的水
融入雾气凝结的河流中。

诗人每日禁锢在家中
出行是为了打破沉静。
出行到一个新家
为了知道自己能够发声。
出行是为了讲话，
对他的话语谁也不会担惊。

是的。成都就是这样的地方，离开它
使人想回来。它是远离家乡的家。

一切都在共谋重返。

多少美事将我们召唤。

多少喉咙。多少听觉。多少对话在等候发声。

成都啊，成都，请将我倾听！

__赵振江/译

Serge Pey

塞尔日·佩里

Serge Pey est né en 1950 à Toulouse d'une mère couturière et d'un père ouvrier du bâtiment réfugié politique de la guerre civile espagnole. Ses années d'enfance marqueront durablement son engagement auprès des mouvements de libération, de résistance et d'éspérance. Tôt, dans son enfance, il entre en contact avec la poésie espagnole et française. Garcia Lorca, Pablo Néruda, François Villion, Rimbaud veilleront sur ses récitations d'écolier. Poète d'action, plasticien, romancier, philosophe du poème, il est l'auteur d'une centaine de publications en France et à l'étranger. Le poète rédige ses textes sur des bâtons avec lesquels il manifeste ses scansions et ses performances. Le prix de poésie Yvan Goll lui a été attribué en 2001. Le prix Guillaume Apollinaire lui a été décerné en 2017.

塞尔日·佩里，法国当代著名诗人。1950年生于图鲁兹。母亲是一位裁缝，父亲是西班牙内战时期的一位政治难民。童年时，他就喜欢上了西班牙和法国诗歌。对洛尔迦、聂鲁达、维庸、兰波等诗人的诗作，他从小就会背诵。他同诗人马查多的瓜葛就更加紧密。他是一位行动诗人，对诗歌进行哲学思考，也搞抽象艺术，还写小说。在法国和其他国家，他已出版一百多部著作。他发明了一种“棍诗”，把诗作写在一条条手臂大小的树干或枝条上，显得既朴素又神秘。首都师范大学中国诗歌研究中心收藏了他当年赠予的一根“诗棍”。他曾获伊凡·戈尔诗歌奖（2001）、阿波利奈尔诗歌奖（2017）。

__树才/译

Fiat Panda

Il y a des jours où rien ne marche
où tout s'écroule
où les chiffons dans les poubelles
se mettent à aboyer
avec des cerfs volants

Ma Fiat panda est rouge
comme un drapeau
mais elle ne ressemble
ni à un panda ni à un ours
ni à un drapeau
pourtant elle a des feux de position
qui la signalent dans la nuit

Il y a des jours où rien ne marche
et où tout s'écroule

Par exemple j'ai crevé ce matin
sur la route de Chengdu
en passant sur un parapluie
ou le clou perdu
par un cordonnier des étoiles

Il y a des jours où rien ne marche
et où tout s'écroule
Ainsi quand j'ai ouvert
le coffre pour prendre ma roue de secours
je constatai qu'on me l'avait volée
sûrement sur le parking de l'hôtel
ou j'avais vu quelques chiens errants
tourner autour de la voiture

Il y a des jours où rien ne marche

et où tout s'écroule

mais heureusement une lune

qui faisait le trottoir sur le parapet

me siffla comme un chien

Cependant je refusais sa proposition

car je ne paie jamais pour cette chose

même si elle belle dans sa robe de cuir

Il y a des jours où rien ne marche

et où tout s'écroule

Mais j'eus soudain l'idée en la voyant si belle

de faire d'elle

une roue de secours

puisqu'elle ressemblait à une roue

même si elle était jaune comme l'or

et mes trois autres roues

étaient noires comme la nuit

Il y a des jours où rien ne marche
et où tout s'écroule
quand avec mon cric
je montais la lune sur l'essieu
je me rendis compte
qu'elle aussi
était crevée
Ses fesses rebondies sous sa robe
ne cachaient qu'un paquet d'os
mais ni un pneu
ni une chambre à air et encore moins une roue
Seulement le dessin d'un lapin et d'un loup
tatoué sur les fesses

Il y a des jours où rien ne marche
où tout s'écroule
Pas de chance vraiment pour la poésie
ma Panda boîte maintenant
et un camion-dépanneur va venir l'enlever
du bas-côté du périphérique où elle stationne
La lune n'avait servi à rien
La morale de cette histoire
est qu'une lune sur un trottoir
ne sera jamais une roue de secours
et que la nuit n'est qu'une odeur
quand elle fait griller des sauterelles
dans la cendre des soleils éteints

Il y a des jours où rien ne marche
et où tout s'écroule

D'ailleurs ce matin j'ai lu
qu'un entrepreneur de Chengdu
certainement un empereur
proposait de faire tourner une seconde lune
artificielle dans le ciel
pour compléter l'éclairage nocturne de la ville
Après réflexion je pense
que c'est lui qui m'a emprunté
la roue de secours de ma Fiat Panda
et que c'est elle qui va désormais briller dans le ciel
à côté de la vraie lune

Chengdu aura ainsi deux lunes
mais personne ne saura jamais
que c'est ma roue de secours volée
qui brillera dans le ciel

et que ce poème est la seule façon

de signaler qu'il y a des jours où rien ne marche

et où tout s'écroule

et que les roues de secours de la poésie

n'existent que dans le ciel

et sûrement pas dans le coffre

des voitures ou des métaphores

qui passent à toute allure sur le périphérique

“菲亚特”熊猫

有几天干啥都不行
一切运转不灵
垃圾堆里的碎布
也开始跟风筝
一起嚷嚷

我的“菲亚特”熊猫
是红色的，像一面红旗
但它既不像一只猫
也不像一只熊
或者一面旗
可是它有火焰
为它在夜里指点方向

有几天干啥都不行
一切运转不灵

比如今天早上我爆胎了
在成都的马路上
我从一顶雨伞下经过
那里有钉子
被星星的鞋匠丢下

有几天干啥都不行
一切运转不灵
因此我打开后备厢
去拿那只备胎
我发现它被偷走了
肯定是在宾馆停车场
我见到几只流浪狗
围着我的车打转

有几天干啥都不行

一切运转不灵

但幸亏有一个月亮

隔着人行道栏杆

狗一样冲我吹口哨

可是我拒绝了她的建议

因为我从不为这种事花钱

即便她的皮裤子挺漂亮

有几天干啥都不行

一切运转不灵

见她这么漂亮

我忽然心生一计

把她做成一只备胎

因为她像一只轮胎

虽说她是金黄的

其他三只轮胎

却漆黑如夜

有几天干啥都不行
一切运转不灵
当我用千斤顶
把月亮上到轴上
我意识到
她也累垮了
她裙子下的肥臀
只藏着一包骨头
既不是轮胎也不是
内胎更不是轮子
只是一只兔子或狼
文身在她的屁股上

有几天干啥都不行

一切运转不灵
诗歌确实没有好运气
我的熊猫现在一跛一拐
一辆拖车将把它掳走
从它停步的环路下边
月亮啥用也没有
这个故事的道德
是一个月亮在人行道上
永远不会是一只备胎
而夜晚只是一种味道
当它把蝈蝈们放在
熄火的太阳灰烬上烤

有几天干啥都不行
一切运转不灵
今天早上我还读到

成都的一位企业家
建议让第二个月亮
在人造天空里运转起来
为了弥补城市的夜间照明
深思之后我想
正是他借给我
“菲亚特”熊猫的那只备胎
而它将照亮天空
在那个真月亮旁边

这样成都有两个月亮
但没有一个人知道
是我那只被偷走的备胎
在天空中闪耀
而这首诗是唯一的方式
说明有几天干啥都不行

一切运转不灵

而诗歌的那些备胎

只在天上存在

肯定不会在汽车

或隐喻的后备厢里

汽车在环路上扬长而去

__树才/译

Shota Iatashvili

邵塔・雅塔什维利

He was born in 1966. He is the author of the 9 collections of poetry and 4 collections of short stories.His works have been translated into English, German, French, Dutch, Russian, Portuguese, Polish, Romanian, Ukrainian, Latvian, Turkish, etc. He has attended many international festivals – ORIENT-OCCIDENT (Romania, 2006), Poetry International (Rotherdam, 2007), Poetry Biennale (Moskow,2007, 2009), BIPVAL (France, 2011) etc. Now he is the editor-in-chief of the literary magazine *Akhali Saunje* and presents the program "Library" on Radio Liberty.

邵塔·雅塔什维利，生于1966年，著有9部诗集和4部短篇小说集。其作品被译为英语、德语、法语、荷兰语、俄语、葡萄牙语、波兰语、罗马尼亚语、乌克兰语、拉脱维亚语和土耳其语等多种语言。他曾参加了包括2006年罗马尼亚东西方学院诗歌节，2007年鹿特丹国际诗歌节，2007年、2009年莫斯科诗歌双年展，以及2011年法国瓦勒德马恩诗歌双年展等各项国际诗歌节。现任《新宝藏》文学杂志主编，并主持自由广播“图书馆”节目。

__唐纳德·瑞菲尔德、刘泽/译

Шота Иаташвили

Инь Си по указанию своего учителя, Лао-Цзи
Искал зелёную козу, нашел его в городе Чэнду
И построил там храм.
А я там вместе со своим японским другом Ясухиро
Нашел зеленое такси и поехал в старый город,
Что-бы прогулятся по древней улице Цзинли
И купить колоду карт со стихами Мао.
В Чэнду огромное стадо зеленых коз,
То есть зеленых такси,
Они все время мелькают перед твоими глазами
И напоминают, что в старые, добрые времена
Лао-Цзи на быке направился на запад и оставил завещание
Искать зелёную козу после тысячи дней практики даосизма.
Я думаю, что это практика
Совсем не похожа на практику Шахерезады,
Которая тянется на один день больше и

Исполняется ночами.

Моя поэтическая практика тоже связана с ночами,

Я ночами пишу стихи и иногда

В своем городе я тоже нередко ищу козу,

Но только белую или черную -

Из своего четвертого этажа

Я спускаюсь вниз, в паб "Kozel" и заказываю его.

Перед пабом часто стоит девочка,

Одетая в костюме козленка

И рекламирует чешского козла.

Год тому назад я в Сичуане познакомился

С чешским поэтом Яромиром,

У которого совсем другая практика:

Он работает в психиатрической лечебнице

И старается там поймать своего козла

И построить храм поэзии –

Написать стихи о том, что поисходит в лечебнице.

В Чэнду я один раз поздно ночью вышел из гостиницы

И начал гулять, осматривать улицы, закоулки, площади.

На одной площади была очень длинная линия

Привязанных велосипедов.

Одна женщина в руке с фонарем освещала номера велосипедов

И передвигалась от одного к другому –

Искала свой велосипед.

Я продолжил прогулку.

Где-то через полчаса я опять попал на той же площади.

Женщина продолжала искать свой велосипед,

Свою козу.

Эта сцена почему-то глубоко запечетлелась в моей памяти

И когда я начинаю вспоминать дни,

Проведенные в Чэнду,

В моем воображении в первую очередь появляется

Не двадцатиметровая фигура Лао-Цзи в храме зеленого козла,

Не спящие панды на деревях

И не облик чэндуйского поэта Ду Фу,

А эта женщина, перед тысячи велосипедов

Исполняющая старое завещание.

青　羊

尹喜根据导师老子给出的教诲，
去寻找一只青羊，在成都找到了它，
并在那里建造了一座宫殿。
我和一位来自日本的朋友康佑
找到一辆绿色的出租车，驶向老城，
为的是逛一逛锦里老街，
买了一副印有毛泽东诗词的扑克牌。
成都有一大群青色的母羊，
还有绿色的出租车，
它们每时每刻在你的眼前闪烁，
提醒那些过去的好时光，
老子骑着公牛向西走，留下遗训，
寻找一只青羊，在道教践行数千天之后。
我想，这样的实践

根本不像山鲁佐德[①]的行为，

她讲的每个故事必须长于每个夜晚，

延长到第二个白天。

我的诗歌行为同样与夜晚密切相关，

每个夜晚我都写诗，有时，

我也同样在城里闲逛，寻找一只羊，

从我的四层楼往下走，

走向招牌“Kozel”[②]，订购一箱啤酒——

但找到的不是白羊就是黑羊。

招牌前面，经常站着一个姑娘，

穿着一件山羊皮的外套，

为捷克产的啤酒大做广告。

一年以前，在西昌，

我结识一位捷克诗人雅罗米尔，

---

① 阿拉伯神话传说《一千零一夜》中的女主人公。

② Kozel 是俄语“公山羊”的发音，也是一种捷克啤酒的商标。

他有的是另外一种行为：

他在一个精神病诊所工作，

努力去捕捉自己的山羊，

建造一座诗歌的宫殿——

他的诗歌描述诊所发生的故事。

在成都，有一次，我深夜走出宾馆，

开始散步，观察街道、小巷子和广场。

我来到某一个广场，那里

排列着一长串的自行车。

有一个女人拿着手电对照着号码，

从一辆自行车查到另一辆——

寻找着自己的自行车。

我继续我的散步。

过了半个小时，我竟然又回到这广场，

那个女人还在寻找她的自行车，

她自己的山羊。

不知怎么的，当我回忆在成都的那些日子，
这一幕留给我很深的印象，
在我的脑海里，首先浮现的，
不是青羊宫里那个二十米高[1]的老子塑像，
不是在树上懒睡的熊猫，
也不是成都诗人[2]杜甫的形象，
而是这个女人，站在上千辆自行车前，
正在践行那个古老的遗训。

__汪剑钊/译

---

① 作者记忆有误，二十米高的应是八卦亭。
② 作者把杜甫看作成都诗人。

Stephen Nashef

史蒂芬·纳什夫

Stephen Nashef is a translator and poet. He was born in Glasgow and currently lives in Guangzhou. His translations have appeared in *Pathlight* and *Tender Buds: 21st Century Chinese Poems*.

史蒂芬·纳什夫，翻译家、诗人，生于格拉斯哥，现居广州。其翻译作品被收录进《人民文学》杂志英文版《路灯》、《初蕾集：新世纪中国诗选》等。

__郑文娟/译

Du Fu Thatched Cottage, Chengdu

It was cold when I was last in Chengdu,
but this time the leaves cling bright
to the tree whose name escapes me –
it is nestled in there somewhere

between spongy roots and tough bark.
I wear my history like a loose-fitting coat,
finely lined and with room enough to squirm in.
But today Chengdu's sun warms my arms

and my coat hangs off a peg on some hotel
room's door. History does its dirty work
on the streets, on the mud pounded hard
beneath hooves, but it is in the quiet

of long evenings in small wooden rooms

under lamplight that it stretches out
on the rug and stares you dead in the eyes
arching its back. Du Fu knew this and so came

to Chengdu, its name sat like a bird on its shoulder:
life in Chengdu is slow, Chengdu people
take it easy. But Du Fu was driven out
of his cottage by mutineers spilling blood

on the streets. Winter and its weather
were nearing when Du Fu made his escape
under the same nameless trees.
It is not known if he remembered his coat.

杜甫用茅草修盖成都草堂

天冷了，我还滞留在成都，
但这时光仍依附在树叶上
树的名字我记不起来了——
它筑巢在海绵状的根

与坚硬的树皮之间的某个地方
我穿着我的历史像一件宽松的外套，
衬里精致，有足够回旋的空间。
但今天成都的太阳晒暖了我的胳膊

而我的上衣悬挂在某个酒店房门的
衣架上。历史在大街上，在马蹄
践踏下的泥浆上从事卑鄙
勾当，但正是在长夜的

安静中，在灯光下的小

木房子里，它躺在地毯上
弓着背直盯着你。
杜甫深知这一点，因此来到

成都，它的名字像一只鸟蹲在它肩膀上：
成都的生活是缓慢的，成都人
很轻松。但杜甫被大街上
制造流血事件的哗变者赶出了

他的草堂。当杜甫从同样
不知其名的树下逃脱时，
冬天和它的严寒正在逼近。
如果他记得自己的外套，它就不为人知了。

—程一身/译

Thierry Renard

蒂埃里·勒纳尔

Est né le 14 août 1963 à Lyon. Ancien élève du Conservatoire d'Art Dramatique de Lyon. Il s'est fait remarquer, dès 1978, dans la région Rhône-Alpes-en tant que comédien, poète et animateur de revue. Il a longtemps partagé sa vie entre l'écriture, le théâtre et de très nombreuses autres activités artistiques. Il est aujourd'hui directeur de l'Espace Pandora à Vénissieux (Rhône), lieu de diffusion et de communication de la poésie. En 2009, il succède à Jean-Pierre Siméon à la présidence de la Semaine de la poésie de ClermontFerrand et il est élu vice-président de l'Agence Rhône-Alpes pour le livre et la documentation. Aujourd'hui, il est le rédacteur en chef de la revue semestrielle RumeurS, actualité des écritures, pour le compte des éditions La rumeur libre. Officier des Arts et des Lettres, promotion du 14 juillet 2013.Œuvres: *Le Fait noir* ,*La Traversée du jour*, *Un monde à l'envers,* etc.

蒂埃里·勒纳尔，法国诗人，1963年8月14日生于里昂。曾就读于里昂艺术学院。早在1978年，他就活跃在罗纳-阿尔卑斯地区（译者注：里昂所在大区）的文学艺术界，既是演员，又是诗人，还编辑出版文学杂志。写作、戏剧和其他艺术活动，占据了他的生活中心。目前他在（罗纳省的）维尼西厄主持一个名为“潘多拉空间”的诗歌文化交流协会。2009年，他接替让-皮埃尔·西蒙担任“克莱蒙-费朗诗歌周”主席，并当选罗纳-阿尔卑斯书籍与文献社副社长。如今，他是“自由言论”出版社文坛时事期刊《喧哗》的主编。2013年7月14日，他获得由法国政府颁发的“艺术与文学骑士勋章”。其主要诗集有《黑色事件》《月亮那玩意儿》《去，呼吸另外的光》《穿越白昼》《反面的世界》等。

__赵文希/译

l'Esprit du Tao

J'avais la nostalgie des ailleurs, non le désir de voyager.

Charles Juliet, Gratitude

À Chengdu
toujours se mélange
les couleurs les saveurs
les grands immeubles gris
les maisons basses des vieux quartiers
les centres d'affaires ou commerciaux
les gens les plus modestes
& les nouveaux riches

À Chengdu il y a
au beau milieu du verre
du ciment et du béton
des espaces verts

des parcs naturels
des musées dont celui
que nous avons visité
un site archéologique
dont les vestiges remontent
à plus de quatre mille ans

À Chengdu
au milieu du bruit
il y a le silence
À Chengdu coulent
des rivières apaisées

Nous sommes en train de vivre
un moment de beauté
impénétrable

Nous sommes entrés soudain
par la grâce
de tous les ciels confondus
dans le repaire du mouvement
FEI FEI (No ! No!)

Nous sommes entrés non
par effraction
mais par un bonheur élémentaire
dans la dernière demeure
habitée par le souffle

Ici c'est le pays du papier
de la calligraphie des idéogrammes
L'esprit du tao flotte
au-dessous des nuages
et l'essentiel est là

道的精神

我怀念别处，却不想旅行。

——夏尔勒·居里埃《感激》

在成都

总是混杂着

各色各味

灰色的大高楼

老街区的矮平房

那些商业中心

那些普通民众

那些新贵

在成都

在漂亮的玻璃

水泥和混凝土之间

有绿色空间

有自然公园
有我们参观过的
博物馆
比如考古博物馆
那些遗迹化石
可以上溯四千年

在成都
在嘈杂声中
有寂静
有平静的溪流

我们正经历
无法穿透的
美妙一刻
我们突然闯入
（感谢时空错乱）

一个运动的巢穴
非非（不！不！）

我们并非
破门而入
而是凭本质的快乐
在人类居住的
最后那个居所

这里是纸的国度
象形文字和书法
道的精神
从云上掠过
本质就在这里

__树才/译

Prose pour Chengdu

De même qu'il y a des livres sur les ruches, sur les cités de nids, sur la constitution des colonies de madrépores, pourquoi n'étudie-t-on pas les villes humaines?

Paul Claudel, Connaissance de l'Est

Au départ, je me suis dit que j'allais écrire un long poème tourné vers cette ville découverte à la fin de l'été 2017. Et puis plus rien n'est venu. Tout est resté en moi enfoui. Là-bas, pourtant, je me suis fait de nouveaux amis, les poètes Shu Cai, Liang Ping et Jidi Majia.

Chengdu ne se visite pas, Chengdu s'explore. Des grandes avenues à la plus petite ruelle, Chengdu se dévoile au fil des heures. Étonnante cité où j'ai perdu mon nom, entre les hauts immeubles et les vastes coins de nature. Chengdu, encore, où j'ai appris à redevenir celui que je fus.

Il y a des jours où l'on désespère un peu de tout. C'est dans le sang que cela se passe. On a trop mangé, trop bu, le sucre de nouveau s'est installé dans le corps. L'humeur, habituellement changeante, devient mauvaise durablement. Un rien vous agace, vous agresse ou, mieux, vous transporte au loin. Tout est écœurant. Malgré la bonne ambiance et le partage. Malgré les rires éclatants et les mains offertes. Malgré la vie qui a le dessus sur chaque chose.

Et, à la maison, l'atmosphère est lourde, on se sent mal accueilli. On est de trop. Et le sucre traverse et retraverse les veines humaines à chaque instant. La tête est lourde, les tempes sont chaudes. Malgré l'hiver qui vient, et le froid au dehors.

On rêve d'innocence, de tendresse totale. On se parle à soi-même. On s'agite en silence, dans l'immobilité du salon. On voudrait prier une bonne fois pour toutes. Mais on ne croit pas. On n'a pas l'horizon assez dégagé devant soi. Pas de perspective claire dans l'au-delà. Tout est tellement prévisible. Tout est terriblement terrestre. Le futur reste méconnu.

Il faudrait faire attention, ne prendre aucun risque, perdre du poids, afin de prolonger l'existence de quelques lignes, de quelques livres, encore... Pour le plaisir des uns et pour le bien des autres. Ce que l'on redoute, par-dessus tout, c'est l'indifférence muette. On voudrait tellement ne pas, voire ne jamais, perdre pied.

Alors, on retourne à Chengdu. Par l'esprit. Par le cœur. Par le corps, aussi. On y est comme chez soi. C'est en Chine, à l'autre bout du monde. Et c'est ici, chez nous. On y est invité. Pour la plus noble des causes. Pour la poésie.

À Chengdu, comme le dit mon ami, le poète Mohammed El Amraoui, il fait doux. Tout est doux, même la douceur de l'air quand, vers le soir, on songe aux nuits d'Orient et à la quiétude absolue. Ici, j'ai déposé tous mes objets familiers sur le grand bureau de la chambre. Et j'ai, sur le sol, posé mes valises.

Tout d'abord, on y a cru. À la beauté sur terre, bien entendu. On a cru notre rêve possible, réalisable. C'est pourquoi il nous a fallu bâtir notre maison et chanter ce qui naît.

Carnaval des grimaçants, corps et visages confondus, liberté grande ou tyrannie du beau... Beauté fatale, beauté du diable, beauté du geste, beauté du monde, beauté des choses, beauté dans l'art, et bien d'autres apparences, encore, multipliées.

Attention, attention, les sources de la Beauté ne sont pas à vendre... Nous ferons tout pour les empêcher de tarir.

Mais il y a tout dans un poème, ou dans une prose poétique. Il y a ce vieux monde réconcilié, apaisé. Il y a la vaste nudité des corps. Alors pourquoi ne pas, voire ne jamais, croire à la beauté du monde et des choses de ce monde ? Comment, d'ailleurs, ne pas croire à toutes ces beautés si différentes ?

Nous n'avons rien voulu éluder. Nous avons voulu tout

dépeindre, et n'échapper à rien de connu ou d'inconnu. Nous avons voulu dire, encore, les mille facettes de la beauté sur la terre. L'exercice fut périlleux, mais le résultat est là, maintenant, très prometteur. L'exercice fut contraignant, en effet, mais tout cela toujours fait partie du voyage.

Un livre, c'est comme une maison, nous l'avons dit, une maison avec un toit, une cheminée, quelques murs, des pièces plus ou moins grandes, des portes et des fenêtres. Une maison d'arrêt ; on y fait halte.

Halte, jusqu'à ce que nos forces d'évocation se libèrent, et se soulèvent…

À Chengdu, les rencontres sont familières et le rire est au rendez-vous. La nourriture est bonne, excellente, même. Et les restaurants sont accueillants. Fourmillants. Et les amis sont nombreux.

Parcs, musées, avenues et immeubles gigantesques, vieux

quartiers et ville moderne, petites boutiques obscures, bibliothèques et librairies, lieux de pèlerinage, lieux saints, lieux finalement magiques. Arbres et rivières. Temples secrets. Tout ici m'a aidé à reprendre mon souffle.

Chengdu, étonnante cité, où j'ai retrouvé un nom, Li Ru.

Et la Beauté, l'éternelle Beauté, dans tout ça ? Elle continue de se consumer dans le poème. Elle apparaît et, aussitôt, elle disparaît.

Attention ! Les sources de la Beauté ne sont plus à vendre. Et l'objet que vous tenez dans vos mains est un livre, un livre ouvert sur le monde.

Je suis à Chengdu, pour l'éternité.

Il y a des jours où Chengdu se ressemble.

le 17 décembre 2018

献给成都的散文

有些书书写蜂巢，书写鸟窝，书写石珊瑚群的结构，为什么我们不对人类的城市也探讨一番？

——保罗·克洛岱尔《认识东方》

我于2017年夏天发现了成都。起初，我想写一首有关这座城市的长诗。然而遥遥无期，一切都埋藏在了心底。不过在那里，我结交了新的友人，诗人树才、梁平以及吉狄马加。

成都不是被游览的，成都是被探索的。从大街至小巷，随着时间流逝，成都在渐渐揭去面纱。在这座令人惊叹的城市里，我徜徉于高耸的楼宇和自然的巨隅间，遗失了我的姓名。在成都，我再一次成为从前的我。

总有一些时日我们有些许灰心，似乎骨子里便是如此颓丧。我们暴饮暴食，糖分也再一次在身体里积聚。情绪起伏不定，也时常久久陷入阴郁。一点鸡毛蒜皮的小事就能刺激你，让你恼火，让你抓狂。一切都令人沮丧：即便有欣悦的氛围以及可分享的趣事，即便有开怀的大笑以及慷慨的援手，即便生活依旧主宰着一景一物。

家里的气氛同样沉重，我们感到不自在，就像是一个多余的人。每一个瞬间糖分都在血管里回溯。即便冬日来临，屋外冰天冻地，脑袋也依旧沉甸甸，太阳穴热烘烘。

我们幻想着单纯以及纯粹的温柔。我们自言自语。我们在寂寥的空房里默默躁动。我们想一劳永逸地祈祷一次，但我们不信神。我们面前没有足够清澈的视野，更远处也没有明亮的前景。一切都如此可预知，一切都如此世俗。未来不可期。

需要留心的是，不要为了去延长几行字、几本书，甚至为了一些人的快乐以及另一些人的利益而去冒险。我们最最忧虑的是不露声色的冷漠，我们不要甚至永远不想失去立足点。

于是，出于精神与心灵所求以及身体所需，我们回到了成都，就像回家了一般。这里是中国，世界的另一端。但这里同样是我们的故乡。我们被邀请至此，为了崇高的理由，为了诗歌。

正如我的朋友，诗人穆罕默德·艾拉·阿姆哈维所言，在成都，天气温柔。一切都温柔。甚至接近夜晚时分，我们怀想东方的长夜和纯粹的静谧时，空气都是温柔的。在这里，我将所有熟悉的物件都摆放在了房间里的大桌子上。我也把我的那些行李箱放倒在地上。

首先，在这里我们有信仰。确信世间的良辰美景，相信梦会开花结果。这就是为何我们需要建造家园以及歌唱新生。

致命的美，魔鬼的美，姿态的美，人群的美，物体的美，美寄居于艺术之中以及其他各色外表之下。

留意啊留意，美的种子并不变卖……我们将竭尽所能遏制它们的枯竭。

不论是诗歌还是散文诗都自有其寰宇。那里有祥和平静的旧地，有庞大赤裸的身姿。然而为什么不相信这世间万物的美？不相信这一切千变万化的美？

我们不曾回避。我们想要描绘一切，不错过任何一个可知或未知的点滴。我们甚至想要传达这世间的千面风华。挑战何尝棘手，然而硕果足以悦人。就算尝试受束，但一切不过是旅途中的插曲。

就像我们所言，一本书如同一栋房舍，有一个屋顶，一根烟囱，几面墙垣，几间或大或小的厅室，几扇门扉以及几帘窗棂。好似一处栖身之地；我们在那里歇歇脚。

我们在那里歇息着，直到回忆有了力度，被释放，被激扬。

在成都，人们相见如故，笑声盈盈填满聚会。玉盘珍馐，色味俱佳。餐馆好客，济济一堂。友人良多。

公园，博物馆，大马路，高楼，老区，新城，书店，图书馆，幽静的小铺，进香的去处，圣杰的灵地，最终都是如此奇异。无论是林野，河水，还是神庙，这一切都助我重获新生。

成都，一座惊奇的城市，在那里我给自己找寻到了一个名字：Li Ru。也找到了美。永恒的美或许就沉醉其中，她倏然重现又稍纵即逝，她在诗歌中绵延耗尽。

留意啊！美的种子不再变卖。你手中所拥有的是一本书，一本敞怀于天地的书。

我永远身在成都。

在成都，有些日子依旧如故。

2018年12月17日

__丁获/译

时间深处的城市

Umberto Mele

翁贝托・梅勒

Umberto Mele is an Italian ex manager of a prominent telecommunication company. He has been living in Chengdu for many years. He has nurtured a profound passion for literature and all form of fine arts since his childhood. During his life he has written hundreds of poems and short stories, many of which have been published on the most important Italian news paper: "Corriere Della Sera" under the pseudonym of Lao Mei.

翁贝托·梅勒，意大利一家著名电信公司的前任经理，现已在成都生活多年。他自幼热爱文学和艺术，写有数百首诗歌和若干短篇小说。他常以笔名“老梅”在意大利重要新闻报纸上发表题名为“童话故事的地方”的系列作品。

__唐为之/译

Eri suadente : fiore di pesco

A Luo Dai

Seduto a un tavolino di un caffè

in una tiepida giornata di marzo

con i pensieri a farmi compagnia.

Col tuo colore

mi facesti alzare la testa per dirmi:

"Sono qui, e tu non mi degni di uno sguardo!"

Ti guardai:

eri vanitosa e da poco sbocciata,

come una adolescente.

Vellutata, color rosa shocking,

inclinata e calma

riposavi di fronte a me.

Tu suadente, ti accorgesti

di avermi sedotto.

Emanasti un profumo

intenso:

come di donna matura;

e diventasti irresistibile.

Ti presi fra le mani e ti dissi:

“Sei magnifica.

Domani vengo in giacca e cravatta,

ti metto in un’ asola e ti porto a

fare un giro.”

桃花：永恒

洛带，一杯夹着午后阳光的咖啡
在阳春里最温柔的三月
我托着双颊望向窗外的你
你绰约的身影勾住了我的魂
我抬起头来，你悄悄对我说：
“我渺如尘埃，不值一顾。”

我看着你
你半掩着含苞待放
宛若豆蔻之年的娉婷少女
奶白的纯情、粉红的娇羞
你静静地斜卧
一不小心在我面前安然入睡

你默默不语
却将我的魂摄去了

你散发着香水般迷人的气息

浓烈而芬芳

又如同风情万种的女人

让我无法抗拒

我把你轻轻放入掌心：

“你如此动人

我要把你别在我的衣襟上

明天，带你去远方。”

__唐为之/译

Yasuhiro Yotsumoto

四元康佑

He was born in Osaka, Japan in 1959 and grew up mostly in Hiroshima. Yasuhiro has been away from Japan since 1986 and living in Munich, Germany. He has published 13 books of poetry. Just recently, two new books of poetry were published simultaneously: *O-MO-TE-NA-SHI: Welcome to Japan* and *Novel*. While his own poems has been translated into more than 20 languages, including book publication in English (*Family Room* by Vagabond Press, Australia), Yasuhiro himself translates works of numerous foreign poets into Japanese. In 2012, Yasuhiro published *Shuntarology*, a thesis on the poetics of Shuntaro Tanikawa. In 2015, his first novel *The Fake Poet* and the collected essays *To Dear Poets*! were published. Since 2006, Yasuhiro has been Japanese national editor of Poetry International Rotterdam, introducing contemporary Japanese poetry through English translations. He is also on the editorial board for the poetry magazine *Beagle* in Japan.

四元康佑，1959年出生于大阪，主要在广岛长大。自1986年起，四元康佑就离开日本，定居于德国慕尼黑。目前已出版13本诗集。近期同时出版两本诗集：《O-MO-TE-NA-SHI：欢迎来日本》和《小说》。他的诗作已被翻译成20多种语言，包括英语版诗集（澳大利亚漂泊者出版社《家庭房间》）。他本人也将众多外国诗人的作品译成日语。2012年，四元康佑对谷川俊太郎诗歌的评论专著《谷川诗学》出版。2015年，他的首部小说《假诗人》和散文集《写给亲爱的诗人》出版。自2006年以来，四元康佑就一直担任鹿特丹国际诗歌节的日本本土编辑，通过英语翻译介绍了很多当代日本诗歌。他同时担任日本诗刊《比格》的编辑。

__西川、王蔚/译

An Ode to a Mosquito

I take the same seat in the same bus for three days.
He is always there,
Stuck flat on the dirty window glass,
Shouting in silence the moment's impact with all His body.

Through him, I see the city for the first time:
The swelling wealth along the street leading to the Panda Breeding Center,
The traffic jam in the rain after visiting Du Fu's house,
Only the way the sky is getting dark remains unchanged since the days of the Three Kingdom.

Hearing absent mindedly the chattering poets with my right ear,
I listened to His silence with my left ear.
It is as vast as the entire territory of this nation, His silence,
Deep enough to swallow all the public slogans on the city streets.

But what separates Him and me is thinner than a pane of glass.
Anybody can go through it given just the right angle,
Into the bubble universe which was crashed together with Him,
And stay there vibrating in the eternal buzzing of His wings.

Li Qing next to me utters a laughter that sounds like 'hu-hi-hu-hi',
Which turns the lights on in the heart on this side of the world.
Through Him, I watch the after image
Of an enormous palm swinging down from beyond the dusk.

成都的蚊子颂

三天来我坐同一辆车同一个座位。
他总在那里，
贴在肮脏的窗玻璃上，
用他整个身体默默地呼喊那一刻的撞击。

通过他，我第一次看见这个城市：
大街膨胀的财富向大熊猫繁育中心延伸，
参观完杜甫草堂后雨中的塞车，
只有天空变暗的方式自三国时代以来保持不变。

用右耳心不在焉地听着诗人的聒噪，
我用左耳倾听他的沉默。
辽阔如这个国家的整个领土，他的沉默，
深得足以吞下这个城市街道上所有的公共标语。

但把他和我隔开的东西比玻璃窗还薄。

只要成直角，任何人都能透视他，
进入那个和他被撞成一体的泡沫宇宙，
停在那里在他翅膀的永恒嗡嗡声中颤动。

挨着我的李清发出大笑声，听起来像“呼嗨呼嗨”，
在世界这边的中心，它震亮了灯。
通过他，我看到从暮色那边
拍下的一个巨大手掌的后来形象。

__程一身/译

Yvon Le Men

伊冯・勒芒

Né en 1953 à Tréguier, est un poète et écrivain français. Son œuvre poétique comporte plus d'une trentaine d'ouvrages. Depuis 1972 il a donné des récitals dans de nombreuses villes de Bretagne, de France et dans une vingtaine de pays. A Lannion, où il vit, il crée, avec Le Carré Magique, en 1992 les soirées "Il fait un temps de poème", où il se fait le passeur des poètes et des écrivains du monde entier. Programmateur aux côtés de Michel Le Bris, il instaure dès 1997 un espace dédié à la poésie au festival Étonnants Voyageurs de Saint Malo. Il est lui même lauréat de nombreux prix dont le Prix Georges Brassens, le Prix de Poésie de l'Académie de Bretagne et des Pays de Loire et le Prix de Poésie Théophile Gautier de l'Académie Française. Poésies: *Le Pays derrière le chagrin, La Patience des pierres suivie de L'échappée blanche,L'Écho de la lumière, Le Jardin des tempêtes, Un Carré d'Aube*, etc.

伊冯·勒芒，法国诗人和作家，1953年出生于布列塔尼的特雷吉耶，著有30多本诗集。自1972年以来，他曾在法国等20多个国家的许多城市举行过诗歌朗诵专场。他生活在布列塔尼地区一个叫拉尼翁的小城。1992年，他与当地的著名的“幻方剧院”合作，发起并组织的名为“诗歌的季节”的系列晚会，成为全世界诗人和作家的交流平台。作为法国作家米歇尔·勒布的合作者，他于1997年在圣马洛“非凡旅人”国际文学电影节中，设置了专门的诗歌单元。他问鼎过诸多大奖，包括“乔治·布拉森奖”、布列塔尼及卢瓦尔河地区学院诗歌奖，以及法兰西学院的诗歌奖“特奥菲尔·戈蒂埃奖”。其主要诗集有《悲伤后面的国度》《石头的耐心（写在白色越狱者之后）》《光的回声》《风暴花园》《一方黎明》等。

__赵文希/译

Du Fu

Hier

dans ma maison au bord du bois

j'ai lu un poème de Du Fu

qui disait

déjà au huitième siècle

L'Empereur n'entend pas le cri de son peuple.

En vain des femmes courageuses ont saisi la bêche et conduis-

ent la charrue ;

Partout les ronces et les épines ont envahi le sol désolé.

et qui dit

encore au vingt et unième siècle

la guerre sévit toujours, et le carnage est inépuisable,

Sans qu'il soit fait plus de cas de la vie des hommes, que de celle des poules et des chiens...

Aujourd'hui

devant la maison de Du Fu

j'ai lu l'un de mes poèmes

sous un ciel en bleu

dans le ciel souvent gris de Chengdu

comme s'il répondait à Du Fu

qui écrivit

le ciel m'envoie une brise compatissante

pour me tenir compagnie

parce qu'il avait écrit

hélas! mon premier chant, déjà

un chant triste

c'est pour ces vers-ci

pour ces vers-là

que sont venus

des hommes

des femmes

comme tout le monde

des empereurs

comme personne

dans la maison de Du Fu

Si je regarde par ses poèmes

je verrai peut-être

ce qu'il a vu

sur le paysage mille fois répété

dans les yeux des passants

mille fois revenus

de tout ce qui fait la vie

depuis toujours

naitre

vivre

mourir

parfois du mauvais côté de la vie

si je regarde par ses poèmes

je verrai sûrement ce qu'il verrait

s'il vivait aujourd'hui

la vie

de la ramasseuse de cartons

du vendeur de kiwis

du rémouleur

de la femme qui porte son restaurant

sur son vélo

la vie

si l'on peut dire

des travailleurs migrants

qui ont monté les villes de la Chine

jusqu'au ciel

dont la nuit se met en quatre
sur une planche de bois

comme partout comme toujours
quand le fleuve de la vie sépare ceux qui vivent
ou ne vivent pas du bon côté du fleuve de la vie

C'est au nom de n'importe quel homme
de sa bonté
parfois

de sa beauté
alors

que nous lisons toujours cet homme

que nous l'aimons

car il a aimé jusqu'à tout perdre

se perdre

jusqu'à inviter dans ses rêves

son rival et son ami

le grand poète Li Bai

J'ai lu un poème de Du Fu

chez moi

j'ai dit un poème de moi

chez lui

malgré les siècles

les pays qui nous séparent

malgré nos langues et grâce à elles

quand elles se font des signes par-delà les nuages

que nous avons regardés

contemplés

lus comme des poèmes qui passent dans le ciel sans limites

sinon celles de nos yeux

杜　甫

昨天
在林边的屋子里
我读到一首杜甫的诗

他写到
八世纪的皇帝
听不见百姓的呼号
勇敢的女人们
徒劳地把锄扶犁
野草和荆棘依然蔓过贫瘠的土地

他还写到
战争肆虐，杀戮不断，
人活得不像人，不异犬与鸡
这些依然发生在二十一世纪

今天

在杜甫草堂

我念了一首自己的诗

在同一片蓝天下

成都的天空常常布满灰迹

好像在回应

杜甫的诗句

他写道：

“悲风为我从天来”

因为，在这一句之前

他还写道：

“呜呼一歌兮歌已哀”

因为这些诗句

因为那些诗句

男人们

女人们

聚到一起

像每一个人

皇上们

不像任何人

聚到杜甫草堂

看他的诗

我也许能看见

他当年所见

千百次重复的风景

行人的目光

他们来来去去

生活的每一个细节

历来如此

出生

活着

死亡

生活也有惨的一面

看他的诗

我肯定能看见他现在所见

如果他还活着

生活——

捡纸板箱的人

卖柿子的人

磨刀的人

还有那位妇女

自行车上搭了个小餐馆

生活——

可以这么说

是那些民工

盖成了大楼

直到摩天

夜间摊开手脚

躺在一块木板上

哪里都一样　从来都一样

当生活之河把人分开

有些人就活在惨的一边

不管以谁的名义

有时是

善的名义

美的名义

我们

一直读这个诗人

我们爱他

他因为爱而失了一切

甚至自己

但他在梦里

还邀请他的对手朋友
大诗人李白

我在我家里
读到一首杜甫的诗
我在杜甫家里
念了一首我自己的诗

尽管隔着世纪
国家把我们分开
尽管语言不同也幸亏语言
词语在云上打着手势

我们看
我们思考

我们读的诗穿越无尽的天空

除非我们的眼睛阻挡

——树才/译

Zdravka Evtimova

兹德拉夫科・伊蒂莫娃

She was born in 1959 in Pernik, Bulgaria. She is a fiction writer and a literary translator from English, German and French. She holds her BA in English language, and MA in American literature from University of Veliko Turnovo, Bulgaria.

兹德拉夫科·伊蒂莫娃，1959年在保加利亚的佩尔尼克出生。她是小说家，也是文学翻译家，主要翻译英语、法语和德语作品；她先后在保加利亚的大特尔诺沃大学获得了英语学士学位和美国文学硕士学位。

__邢小何/译

Every Street in Chengdu Is a Poem

Every street in Chengdu is a poem.
The faces you see, quiet, smiling, sad or happy
tell you stories that you can read
with your heart.
A girl waiting in front of a shoe shop,
glancing every now and then at her telephone,
glancing again
and again and
no one comes.
The face of this girl is small and narrow.
Her dark eyes
are a sky hat has lost its moon.
And at that moment, her mobile phone is
a desert that offers no direction and no help.
The girl looks around and then
glances at her mobile phone

one more time.
The darkness falls
like a bird that cannot find its nest.
The breeze is warm
and impatient
like the darkness in the girl's eyes.
Then bus Number 21 stops
not far from the shoe shop.
A young man, a very ordinary guy -
dark hair, dark eyes -
jumps out of the bus.
He looks around.
There is no one waiting for him
at the bus-stop.
He speaks a few hurried words into his telephone
and a girl with a small and narrow face

goes out of the shoe shop.
I remember her well.
The boy tells her a few words.
I do not speak Chinese,
but I think these must have been
the softest, the kindest words
in the Chinese language.
The eyes of the girl
that have lost the moon and the sky
suddenly light up.
Her face glows.
The darkness
around the boy and the girl turns
into a morning in September.
I do not speak Chinese
although I like so much its melodious rich flow,

but I could read the beautiful poem that
the small shoe shop in Chengdu
whispered in my ear.
In the autumn,
Chengdu is a poem
about a happy girl
with a narrow glowing face.

成都的每条街都是一首诗

成都的每条街都是一首诗。
你看见的那些脸，平静的，微笑的，悲伤的或快乐的
无不向你透露你可以用心读懂的
故事。
等候在鞋店前的一个少女，
不时瞄一眼她的手机，
再瞄一眼
又瞄一眼
还是无人到来。
这个少女的脸小而长。
她的黑眼睛
是消隐了月亮的天空。
这时，她的手机是个
荒漠，既不提供方向也不提供帮助。
这个少女环顾四周，又
一次瞄向

她的手机。

夜幕降临

像一只找不到巢的鸟。

微风暖暖的

那么不耐烦

像这个少女眼中的黑暗。

随后21路公交车

距这家鞋店不远处停下来。

一个青年人，很普通的小伙子——

黑头发，黑眼睛——

从车里跳出来。

他环顾四周。

公交站

没人等他。

他匆忙朝手机里说了几句话

一个瓜子脸的少女

从鞋店走出来。

我清楚地记得她。

那男孩对她说了几句话。

我不会说汉语，

但我想那必定是

用汉语说的

最温柔，最体贴的话。

少女的那双眼睛

本来月亮已消隐，天空

突然亮了。

她的脸泛起红晕。

那男孩和少女周围的

黑暗

变成了九月的清晨。

我不会说汉语

尽管我很喜欢它的悦耳流畅，

但我能读懂这首美丽的诗

成都那家小鞋店

在我耳畔的低语。

在这个秋天，

成都是一首诗

其核心是一个红润长脸的

快乐少女。

—程一身/译

Анна Анатольевна Золотарева

安娜・佐洛塔列娃

Родилась 3 июня 1978 году в Хабаровске, русский поэт и переводчик.Окончила психологический факультет Хабаровского института искусств и культуры.В 2004 году переехала в Москву и поступила в Литературный институт им. А.М. Горького, в котором проучилась два года. Стихи начала писать с двенадцати лет.Публиковала стихи в журналах «Октябрь», «Футурум Арт», «Журнал ПОэтов», «Пролог» и др., в китайской антологии современных русских поэтов.

安娜·佐洛塔列娃，1978年6月3日出生于哈巴罗夫斯克，是俄罗斯诗人、翻译家，毕业于哈巴罗夫斯克艺术与文化学院的心理系。2004年他移居莫斯科，同年开始了为期两年的高尔基文学院学习生涯。他从12岁开始写诗。其作品主要发表在《十月》《未来世界展示艺术》《诗人》《序幕》等刊物。有作品被收入在中国出版的《当代俄罗斯诗选》。

__汪剑钊/译

В Китае Спозараночку

В Китае спозараночку
в горячечном чаду
влюбиться в китаяночку
из города Чэнду
в её ладони узкие
в лукаво-детский взгляд
какого девы русские
ни в жизнь не повторят

великая провинция –
перцовый Сычуань
где силилась сплотиться я
в единый инь и ян
здесь девушки красивые
от влаги говорят
как лотосы красивые –
их на обед едят

где между лотофагами
став тоже лотофаг
мира под флагами
иду сбивая шаг
сместилось мироздание
смешались ты и я –
здесь недопонимание –
основа бытия

чтоб не свихнуться в лёгкую
с гриппозного ума
цитату гумилёвскую
верчу и вдруг сама
разверзнулась усмешкою
внесущностная дверь –
входи в неё не мешкая
но ничему не верь!

大清早在中国[①]

大清早在中国
冒着窒闷的热气
爱上一个中国姑娘
她来自成都
爱上她纤瘦的手掌
孩子似的调皮眼神
这样的姑娘俄罗斯人
一辈子都不会碰上

一个伟大的省份——
胡椒味弥漫的四川
我竭尽全力去贴近
那个完整的阴与阳
人们常说这里的

---

① 原诗无题，取第一行为题目。——译者注

姑娘因为湿润而美丽
就像美丽的莲花——
午餐时被人们食用

置身在食莲人中间
我也成了食莲人
在和平的旗帜下
我的步子有点散乱
宇宙因此被颠倒了
你和我混淆在一起
这里的不明之处——
就是存在的基础

为了不致因为感冒
变得失态而不拘礼节
我本人突然摆弄

古米廖夫的引文

一扇非现实的大门
迸裂如同一丝讪笑——
不要磨蹭赶紧进去
但你对什么都别相信！

__汪剑钊/译

时间深处的城市

Вячеслав Куприянов

维雅切斯拉夫·格列波维奇·库普利雅诺夫

Вячеслав Куприянов was born in Novosibirsk in 1939. He graduated in 1967 from the Moscow Linguistic University. He is a freelance writer, a member of Russian and Serbian Writers Unions, of Russian PEN. He is living in Moscow.

维雅切斯拉夫·格列波维奇·库普利雅诺夫，1939年出生于新西伯利亚。1967年，他毕业于莫斯科外语学院（现更名为“莫斯科语言大学”）。他是一名自由写作人，是俄罗斯和塞尔维亚作家协会的会员，也是俄罗斯笔会的会员。他现居住于莫斯科。

__汪剑钊/译

Чэнгду

В городе поэтов и белых панд
В китайском городе Чэнду
Я увидел, где жил поэт Ду Фу,
Где поэт Ду Фу вспоминал поэта Ли Бо
И теперь. вспоминая поэта Ли Бо,
(Я стал писать стихи, читая Ли Бо)
Я вспоминаю поэта Ду Фу
И вспоминаю город Чэнду,
Где я познакомился с новыми поэтами,
Поэтами Китая и всего мира,
И мой мир стал от этого шире –
Спасибо тебе, город Чэнду!

成　都

在一座诗人之城和熊猫之城，
在一座中国的城市——成都，
我看到诗人杜甫曾经居住的地方，
诗人杜甫曾经在那里忆念诗人李白。
而今天，一想到诗人李白，
（我一边阅读李白的诗，一边写诗）
我就会想起了诗人杜甫，
我就会想起成都这座城市，
我在那里结识新的诗友，
那些来自中国乃至全世界的诗人，
我的世界因此而变得更加广阔——
谢谢你，成都这座城市！

__汪剑钊/译